A MEMORY'S WEB

A Conspiracy Unveiled

Chris Witt

TABLE OF CONTENTS

CHAPTER 1
LOST IDENTITY

The first thing I noticed was the tortuous pain on the left side of my face. It wasn't clear if the nausea curling in my stomach was from that or if it was connected to whatever was making my face wet. I tried opening my eyes, but only the right one would cooperate—and it could only show me a blurry mess of books piled together on the floor across from me.

Why the fuck was I on the floor? I tried to remember, but all I got was an urge to vomit. The term *retrograde amnesia* sprang to mind. Based on the throbbing pain, something had seemingly tried to cave in the side of my head and left me with nothing.

I forced myself to sit up and immediately felt dizzy—a sign that I had a concussion. I needed medical attention, but the thought of calling an ambulance was met with dread. "Taking care of it myself then."

Raising my hand to my head, I found that the wetness I'd felt wasn't blood but some mix of tears and snot. Whatever had hit me hadn't torn off half my face, at least. All I needed was to get something for the swelling and something else that would stop me from wanting to rip my head off to stop the pain.

Looking around the room, there wasn't a lot I could use. Besides the different stacks of books, there was a raggedy bed with its cover all bunched up. I prayed that the large sticky splotch covering part of the wooden floor was some weird design choice and not related to the knocked-over cans or rancid smell in the air, but I knew I wouldn't be so lucky. Whatever that stuff was, it didn't bode well for my chances of finding something clean nearby.

The only way out of the room was through one of the two doors on the right wall; I figured that no matter how bad a place this was, there had to be a bathroom, and one of these doors would lead to it. While the white paint was chipping from both, the door handle on the leftmost one was barely hanging on. Figuring it was a sign of use, I took my chance with the nearly broken path.

The room on the other side was larger than the one I had come from. It formed an L-shape, which had been divided up into a living room near the bedroom and a sad, makeshift kitchen near what seemed to be the front door. The space was more well-kept than the bedroom, which made it obvious somebody had torn the place apart looking for *something*.

As much as I wanted to do my own digging, I knew I had to take care of myself first. There wasn't a lot to the kitchen; a fold-out table was set up with a microwave between an old, white fridge and another door—one that, given its placement, would probably lead to the same place as door number two from the bedroom. Several clear containers were scattered around the floor alongside a variety of canned foods. Someone had gone through them all. The fridge was a little more useful. I grabbed one of the bags of mixed vegetables and placed it on my head.

I hissed at the cold and quickly removed it. The thin layer of plastic wasn't enough to protect my skin. And I still needed to see the damage.

"Where is that fuckin' bathroom?"

I didn't have to wait long to find the answer. Past the extra door was exactly what I was looking for. The toilet and shower were set up on the left wall, the door to the dump known as a bedroom was across the way, and on the right was the sink, mirror, and medicine cabinet that I'd been hoping for.

Throwing the veggies in the sink, I quickly assessed myself. My hair was a dark brown and on the longer side with the left half being clumped together. Turned out I had bled but my hair had stopped it from spreading all over the place. Although my skin was white, it didn't seem too pale, so I likely had little internal bleeding. The worst part was the swelling and bruising. The area above my left eye and temple was about double the size it probably should have been and was already starting to turn a dark purple.

Thankfully, the medicine cabinet was well stocked: a large variety of pills, bandages, antiseptic wipes, and even some bruise cream.

Popping three pills—two for pain and one for nausea—I quickly got to work. Getting the blood out of my hair was easy until the small cut started to bleed again, dotting my face, shirt, and floor before I could get one of the bandages to stay in place. The cream had a sharp, medicinal smell to it that was almost as agonizing as the need to rub it into my skin. A quick check at the label told me it was best to leave the cream untouched for 20 minutes, meaning I had to leave the frozen veggies behind.

With the wound taken care of, I quickly ran through the place and turned off all the lights. The room was completely dark with no windows, but that was better for my head. Once done, I found myself in the living room area with my back pressed against the sofa. I wasn't sure why I'd sat there or why my hands felt the need to play with the little flap of fabric that covered the space between the bottom of the couch and the floor—it had just felt right.

"Guess that's as good a place as any to start," I muttered to myself.

I was the type of person to sit on the floor. My hands preferred to be moving. I had some decent medical knowledge. And, if this place was mine, I needed to get my shit together. I was lean, but something told me I was strong. Then there was the face I'd seen in the mirror; something about the way I looked had felt wrong, but I couldn't tell if it was because of the giant lump or not.

Then there was my name. No matter how hard I thought, all I could think of was something with a D or maybe a J? Unless I wanted to go around as "DJ," I needed to find my ID. A quick check of my pockets only gave me some receipt for a large black coffee from a place called "Corners." The rough image of a small little café with gross food came to mind. It wasn't a lot, but someone there might know me.

I was weighing the pros and cons of getting up when I heard something. The sound was faint but unmistakable—someone had unlocked the front door.

I rolled under the sofa by instinct. It was a bit of a tight squeeze, but I was sure that my whole body was covered. I had just enough time to wonder if that was what caused me to want to sit on the ground when the door opened.

From the footsteps, I could tell there was only one person. It was too dark for me to see them as they quickly made their way around the place: first, the kitchen, then past me in the living room, and finally, a quick look around the bedroom and bathroom. It was only after this sweep of the place that they turned on the lights.

Whoever it was wore a pair of dark, navy jeans that seemed too big on them. Their shoes were brown leather and looked clean save for the small red splotch on the side leaving a small trail behind them as they walked. They were trailing blood. They were trailing *my* blood.

I held my breath as they got closer to the couch. My heartbeat in time with their steps. As good a place as this was to hide, it left me with no way to defend myself. All I could do was watch. They got closer to the sofa. I could hear them moving stuff around.

And then they moved toward the bedroom. A part of my brain screamed at me to make a run for it, but I pushed it down. Even with all the pills I took, I was still too unsteady on my feet. Running would only get me caught. Plus, the person had finished in the living room, so they likely wouldn't search it again. It should be safe to stay here, to listen, and to try and figure out more about the situation.

I didn't know how long they stayed in the bedroom, but I could hear things being thrown around. The sound died down and was quickly replaced with what I could only guess were the cupboards being opened in the bathroom. That second search was a lot shorter and ended with a faint ringing sound. The person was calling someone.

"He's not here." The voice, a man's, was deep and sounded like it had had ten too many cigarettes. "Looks like he scattered." There was a small pause and then the man was speaking again. "Got it."

The front door opened and closed. I stayed where I was. I had no way of knowing if the person had left or if they were waiting for me to reveal myself. Ten minutes went by, and then 20 minutes. It was only after almost half an hour had passed that I shimmed out of my hiding place.

Whoever that man had been was searching for someone—a man. As much as I'd have loved for it to be a coincidence, I knew it was probably me. That meant that, as disgusting as the bedroom was, it might have clues to my lost identity.

The room was worse now. The books were covering the floor, making it almost impossible to navigate. It seemed like the man had focused on those. But none of the chemistry books or brochures filled with maps and the history of Gamorah city—the cesspool that we lived in if that itch in the back of my head was right—held what that man wanted.

Based on how each page had been highlighted and scribbled on, it must have been important at some point. Now, though, the words were almost an ancient language in my eyes. Whatever past-me had come up with was lost along with everything else.

I looked around the room again. The man had searched the place, but I'd only heard the books being thrown. Based on how he missed me in the living room, he hadn't bothered to search beyond the surface. My best bet would be the bed.

It didn't take long to remove the covers and pillows from the pile they'd been left in, but that little bit of effort was rewarded. Stuck in the covers was a fake nail for a pinky that had been painted a dark purple color. It wasn't mine, and I doubted it was from the man who'd been in here earlier. That meant there was someone else—hopefully not some partner that would get pissed at me for not remembering them.

Besides that, the bed was empty; there wasn't even a slit along the bedding or mattress to hide something. But there had to be more. If this was my place, and I didn't already have them on me, then I'd have had to have put my wallet or keys somewhere.

My eyes landed on the floor and the gross stains that covered most of it. It was disgusting and at odds with the rest of the place. Well, the apartment was rundown, there had been no stains anywhere else in the house. And if current-me hated it, then past-me did too. So why would I have left it?

"Please be right."

I ran my hand over the sticky floorboards and felt it shift. A little more pressure and the board popped up, revealing a small space underneath with a black leather wallet and gray lanyard with five keys attached. I'd found it, the first clues to who I was.

CHAPTER 2
SHADOWY PURSUIT

"Jacob Hunter," a 43-year-old man who lived at 89 Filthments Street. The driver's license was new but beat up. If I could drive, that meant that I probably had a car somewhere parked out front. Unfortunately, the lanyard hadn't come with a clicker.

I walked around another one of the cars, hoping I didn't look too suspicious as I tried what seemed to be the car key for the tenth time. Again, the key didn't fit. I was about ready to go toward the eleventh car when I heard someone clear their throat behind me.

Turning around, I came face-to-face with a police officer. My stomach sank. Even though the uniform was too big for him, the man—Office Duncan—was intimidating. His brown eyes seemed too wide and worked with his wild blond hair to give him an unsettling appearance.

But his brown leather shoes caught my attention. Something about them felt off.

I figured it would be better to greet the man. "Officer."

"Interested in explaining what you were doing?"

I frowned at his voice. It sounded off. It was almost like he was trying to speak in a higher decibel than normal but could barely manage it past his smoker's lungs.

There was a red spot on one of his shoes.

Shit.

Forty minutes hadn't been enough.

"I, uh," I stumbled over my words as I took in his appearance. While the handcuffs, pepper spray, and baton were firmly attached to his belt, the holster was open. He was ready to shoot. "My girl asked me to get something from her car."

Duncan's hand shifted, leaving me no choice but to act. I kicked him in the groin. As he leaned forward, I grabbed his head and wrenched my knee up. The cracking sound rang through the air a second before the blood started cascading out of his nose. I kneed him again, just to be safe, then grabbed the gun.

He tried grabbing my arm, but he was too unbalanced to be a threat. I forced him to the ground and sent another kick to his crotch before bolting.

I only made it a couple of cars down when I felt a weight against my back. My right forearm hit the pavement first, followed quickly by my knees. The blunt pain quickly subsided, letting me feel each edge that the rocky pavement was pushing into me. It hurt like hell, but it supported my upper body.

Then, the arm went around my neck. My instincts kicked in. I threw my head back, smashing against the already broken nose, when I forced the left half of my body up. The weight rolled off me. I let the momentum carry me further until I was facing Duncan, the gun resting against his forehead.

The two of us stared at each other. Both of us were waiting for the other to move. But what broke the spell was the scream from over by the apartment door. It hit me what the scene looked like: a man with a swollen face and blood-covered clothing pointing a gun at an officer.

Any chance I had to question the man was gone. I needed to leave. I quickly whipped the back of the gun into his forehead before grabbing the handcuffs on his belt. A second later, I had one of his hands attached to a car door. He wouldn't be able to follow me now and any officers called to the scene would probably focus on helping their friend before going after me.

Making sure the safety on the gun was on, I slipped it under my shirt and ran.

***

I'd gotten lucky with how late in the day it was. The sun had set soon after I'd made my escape. The streets, filled with shops, restaurants, and bars, were dark and filled with people. It would be nearly impossible for the police to find me.

Unfortunately, nearly impossible didn't seem to apply to everyone. Some man in a large black hoodie had followed me as I walked. I chalked it up to a coincidence at first and started varying up my route, but he copied each turn and even the pace I was going.

If I knew any shortcuts, they weren't coming back. That meant that I couldn't get away. My only option was to corner the hooded man and confront him. I checked each alleyway we passed, looking for any that were at least somewhat vacant. When I finally found one, I made my way toward one of the walls and leaned my shoulder against it, my hands positioned carefully behind my back.

The hooded man froze for a second when he rounded the corner and saw me. But the hesitation quickly went away, and soon he was walking over to lean against the wall opposite me. He seemed relaxed, wearing an easy smile on his face.

"Hey, Hunt. Been a while."

I licked my lips. He knew me. That could have been why he was following me. But his hands were behind his back in the same way mine were.

I figured it would be best to play it safe. "Did you need something?"

"Not really." His smile shifted, a hint of sadness appearing on his face. "Just want to remember the moment."

"Why? Do you think something's going to happen?" I let my hands drop so the gun was rested against my side.

"Ha, see, that"—the hooded man mimicked my movements, confirming my suspicions that he was armed—"was the reason you were my favorite."

"Not anymore?"

"Don't get me wrong. I still like ya better. But orders are orders."

So, someone really was out to get me. "Sure, we can't just go our separate ways?"

He laughed. "Your face isn't that pretty."

It seemed like he was moving in slow motion. The gun arched upward to point at my head. It would have been a quick death. But his mercy gave me the moment I needed. It didn't matter where I hit.

The bullet went into his knee, throwing him off-kilter and causing his shot to miss. I rushed forward and reached for the gun. I expected resistance, but he didn't fight back as I took it. All he did was offer me a small, pained smile.

Crouching down, I forced his hoodie off and threw it to the ground beside me. He laughed. His voice when he spoke was shaky but still full of the same confidence he had earlier. Though he'd put it up in a bun, strands of his dirty-blond hair had fallen into his face. "And I thought you already took your shot."

I rolled my eyes before starting to remove his shirt. His torso was littered with scars. Along the right side of his chest was a black spiral that formed a path for the many black dots to follow outward. Somehow, I knew exactly what it meant. It was a gang symbol. One, two, twelve dots—one for each of his kills. The more dots, the more respect you had among the Droguers.

But I couldn't focus on that. Not when he was bleeding out. "Keep it wrapped up and put pressure on it. As long as the bullet didn't fracture, you should be fine."

"Oooh, we are playing patient and doctor, now?"

I ignored him. After I tightened the shirt around his knee as best as I could, I grabbed his hands and brought them to the wound.

"The police should be here soon. They'll be able to get you taken care of. Just don't die until then."

"Maybe I will. Just to spite you." I rolled my eyes one last time before grabbing the discarded hoodie and standing up. I only got a few steps away when he spoke up again. "I expect that back later!"

I hummed in response, even though he probably couldn't hear it. When the alley ended, I put on the hoodie. It was a decent fit and did a perfect job of hiding my swollen face—the smell of weed clinging to it was the only downside.

With both guns hidden away, I melted back into the crowd of people. I'd need to double my distance from the cops and move in a different direction before I could settle down for the night. While no one cared about me now, any security camera could have picked up what happened. All they'd have to do was connect this incident with the one from the parking lot and then the search would be renewed—with a whole new vigor to boot.

The area I ended up in was a park in the nicer, residential part of town. Fewer cameras tracked my every movement, though any passing person would be far more judging. There was a fifty-fifty chance on whether any random passerby might ignore the homeless man or call the police to get the "stain" removed from their pristine neighborhood.

Still, it was the best bet for me—if only for a little while. The area having more funding meant there were some water fountains, and I was desperate for a drink. The wallet I'd found had money in it, but it would be best to save that; if I were going to stake out that Corners café place, I had the receipt for, then I'd probably need to show up as a customer.

The water was, thankfully, cold. That meant that it would work for the second thing I had in mind. The pain pills had long since worn off and I had brought none of that bruise cream with me when I left the apartment, let alone any ice. But if I wet my shirt and kept the dirtier parts away from the bandaged wound, then the swelling should at least go down a little.

I jogged off a little ways away from the path so I wasn't directly in the light; the last thing I needed was a public indecency charge. But there was still enough light where I stopped that I saw it. Tattooed along the right side of my chest was a black spiral with three dots.

I killed three people.

Out of everything, that was what made me almost puke. It made sense, in a way. I was too sure of myself in a fight. I had hidden my own shit in the apartment and had way too many medical supplies. But I'd barely let myself think about if I was a bad person—let alone if I was a murderer. Three people dead, because of me. And wasn't three all you needed to be considered a serial killer?

That thought was enough to make me throw up.

That thought was enough to make me throw up.

CHAPTER 3
THERAPY SESSION

The food at Corners was as bad as my vague memory suggested it would be. While the English muffin was okay, the sausage inside was burnt on the outside yet had shards of ice in the middle. The cheese that they stuck on top was almost plastic, but it had been at least 12 hours since I'd had anything and anything I'd eaten before the memory loss was now in the grass of that park.

It had taken me a while to get moving after that. Most of the night had been a blur. But in the morning, I'd woken up with a face full of dirt, an ache in my back that rivaled the one on my face, and considerably less swelling—not to mention a ravenous stomach. Killer or not, I still needed to eat.

Corners hadn't been hard to find once I was back in the shopping district. The buzzing in my brain made thinking hard, which meant muscle memory could take over. Letting myself walk was all it took to get to the café. Two large windows took up most of the front wall of the building; the only space they had for the name was on the green front door, where they'd painted it in yellow, on an angle.

The interior decorating wasn't much better. Army -green paint covered the barren walls and, when paired with the walnut floors, made the whole place feel dark. The larger booths near the window weren't too bad, thanks to the natural lighting, but the same couldn't be said for the small, one-person tables in the back. Anyone who sat there would be hidden from the world—which was exactly why I'd sat there.

With no phone, computer, or even a radio, I had no way of knowing what the media was saying about me. They might have been blasting my face around, hoping someone would call a sighting in. Or maybe I was just being paranoid.

Either way, I had to be careful as I tried to find out more about myself. The café had been a bust. When I'd asked the woman behind the counter if she remembered me, she'd guessed my name. Had she been close, it might have been something, but "Adam" and "Jacob" were about as far away from each other as possible. So, while I'd come here in the past, it either wasn't often or with enough presence to be remembered.

As I was musing about what to do next, a to-go cup was placed on my table by an incredibly skinny woman. Whoever it was, she clearly wasn't a worker. She wore a short, tight black dress with fishnet stockings and an oversized purple zip-up sweater tattered from use. Sticking out of one of her pockets was a pair of red high-heels and, in the other, a red clutch. As I stared at her, she tied her long black hair into a messy bun. Even though she held herself with confidence, I couldn't help but notice how young she seemed.

Eventually, I accepted that she would not talk first. "Can I help you?"

She stared at me for a second, searching for something. Whatever she saw made her smile. "Ya could say 'thanks' for the drink."

I looked at the foam cup. Like hell, was I going to drink it. Instead of distrust, the woman seemed to take my actions as hesitation. She pulled a chair from the table next to mine and sat down across from me.

"Listen. We should talk"— she pointed at the bruises on my face— "about that."

She looked around the room, nervously. It suddenly hit me that she was treating me like glass, like someone she didn't know how to approach me without setting me off. But she had come up to me and given me a drink—out of pity?

My stomach twisted as a thought popped into my head. "No, no. You've got it all wrong. I'm not being abused."

She stared at me for an uncomfortable long amount of time. Finally, she nodded. Taking out her clutch, she pulled out a beaten-up business card and slid it across the table. "Alright. How 'bout this? I'll call and let 'em know ya're coming and need to talk ta Kathy."

Before I could turn her down, the woman—Edith based on the name on her cup—tapped the card with her acrylic nail and left, her phone already to her ear. I dragged both the cup and card toward me, giving them a once-over.

K. Law

Clinical Therapist ○ Licensed Psychiatrist

I didn't know what a clinical therapist did, but I knew that they worked with the mind. If anyone could help with my memories, it would be them.

***

The office was dull. While the cream walls had a lot of paintings, they were all plain. In the room, an oak cube served as a table, holding tissue boxes, candies, and scented candles. It was only thanks to the cushion on the orange sofa being so misshapen that the place didn't seem like a showroom. A part of me hated it and felt like there was something wrong, but the plain and inoffensive look was probably purposeful; it would be easy to get someone to open with no distractions.

Dr. K, or Katherine as she had introduced herself, stood near a small table next to the door, and a filing cabinet where she was making some tea. Her white blouse and black skirt combo were about as plain as the room—there wasn't even any jewelry to give me a hint about her personality. The only thing about her that wasn't perfectly in place was the brown roots coming in from her blonde hair. She was just average, and that set me on edge.

Still, I was here and had no leads. If there was even a chance she could help me, it was worth a shot.

She handed me one of the two cups before sitting down across from me. "So, Jacob, let's start with what you know."

"None of this leaves the room?"

"Client confidential promises that anything said to a therapist will not be told to anyone else without permission."

I stared at her for a second, trying to judge if she was being truthful. "Unless you deem me a threat to myself or others."

"Do you think yourself a threat?"

I winced. "I think... I was part of a gang."

"That doesn't mean you're dangerous. Sometimes, people are put into tough positions."

The two guns I still had hidden under my shirt and the three dots that felt like they were burning my skin suggested otherwise. "Right."

"And not everyone in a gang is dangerous. There are many roles. You could be a runner, a sex worker. You could... work with drugs."

My mind flashed back to the piles of chemistry books that had coated the bedroom floor I'd woken up in; it would fit with drug making.

"Do you know anything about Droguer?"

Kathrine smiled. "More people than you'd think ask me that. From what I hear, about ninety percent of the drug problem Gamorah has stems from them. They make it themselves. Is that the group you were with?"

"Maybe."

"Then, perhaps we should talk about how the group works—it may jog your memory. From what I understand, most of them use two different homes. One is for meeting with

other Droguers and doing work, while the other is for more—
"

"Personal affairs." I thought about the keys: one was to the apartment I woke up in, one to a car, and one of the last two was to another place. Another home that was far away from the first. A nicer place in the residential part of town.

When I looked up, I noticed Katherine sitting at the edge of her seat. I glared at her. "How do you know so much?"

"Sorry, Jacob, client confidentiality." Her expression didn't waver. She was as calm as she had been when I first walked in. That unnerved me even more.

"I think I'm done here."

"Are you sure, Jacob? I just want to help."

"No, no, it's okay." I stood up and hurried toward the door. I couldn't get out of the office faster if I tried.

Chapter 4
Fragments of the Past

The second apartment was a small house in the same neighborhood as the park I'd ended up in the night before. In hindsight, the proximity to "home" might have been the only reason no one had called the police—they all believed I belonged there.

Like the neighborhood, this home was a lot fancier than the first. Even the air was nicer thanks to the multiple plug-in air fresheners sending out spurts of "ocean breeze." The front door led to a small entryway before opening into an open-concept space. The lounge part was fitted with several oak bookcases, a TV, and a light blue couch which rested against the counter that served as the marker for the start of the kitchen. The countertops were made of what looked like polished stone, and the appliances seemed new and hardly used. Despite the lack of use, there was every tool you could imagine for cooking stored away in the drawers: a garlic press, mortar and pestle, and even a fucking oyster knife.

Past that was the bedroom. It had the same blue-gray color scheme as the front of the house. The bed was queen-sized and placed in the center of the room, with two bedside tables on either side. There was a desk set up in the corner next to the closet. And, best of all, an end suite bathroom with a large tub and a first aid kit with enough supplies it could contend with the stuff from the first apartment.

I took my time getting cleaned and patched up. I felt safe here. After everything, it was nice to relax.

With a clean outfit and a cup of decaf, I sat down on the sofa to collect my thoughts. I was getting a vague idea of who I was. My name was Jacob Hunter, and I was a member of Drogue. I was tied up in their drug operation, which led me to have decent medical and fighting experience. I'd killed three people. And the gang wanted me dead; plus, the fact that the police were after me.

I took a sip of my coffee and coughed it up. "And apparently, I can only afford stuff that tastes like ass."

Taking the cup to the sink, I dumped the full thing out. As I did, I took in the look of the sink. It and the counter— every part of the place really—was nearly spotless. The place didn't seem like it had been recently cleaned; a few checks around showed a couple of areas with a fine layer of dust. It was as if no one lived here. But it was well stocked, and all the clothes in the closet fit me.

So then, it was likely this was another throw-away residence, and the last key went to what was my *actual* home. "With all that rent, it's no wonder I can't afford anything that actually tastes good."

I looked around the place again, this time looking for any oddities. Past-me had used a stain to point toward his hiding place before at the apartment, but it didn't seem like I'd used the same technique here.

The books were my first stop. I removed each one from its place on the shelf and shook out the pages to see if there was anything hidden inside. While a couple of the books had been hallowed out, they held nothing. The oak paneling wasn't hiding anything, either.

I'd been about to enter the bedroom when I stopped and glanced at the couch. There had been nothing under the one in the first apartment, but my instincts had directed me to hide there. And had I found anything over the last few hours, it was that my instincts were sharp. Feeling around underneath the sofa, I found something soft.

It took a little while, but eventually, I'd managed to get a duffle bag free. Opening it up, I found a large supply of yellowish-white powder divided into clear plastic baggies. It looked like old sugar. But, without a lab, there was only one way to tell for sure.

The little bit I put on my tongue tasted disgusting; it was overwhelmingly bitter and clearly chemical. Rushing to the sink, I immediately tried spitting it out. It took washing my mouth out twice to finally get the taste to go away.

As I stood hunched over the sink, one word kept replaying in my head: *Molly*.

It had only been a minuscule amount, and it was only there for a moment, so it shouldn't affect me, but the thought still turned my stomach. I'd need water before I continued my search of the place. Any plans I had to take pain pills were also thrown out the window if I wanted to be sure that I didn't make a dangerous mix.

The only bright side was this confirmed that I worked closely with drugs before I got nearly beheaded.

Grabbing the duffle bag, I moved to the bedroom and continued my search. I skipped searching for loose floorboards, figuring that the place was too well-kept for something like that. Instead, I focused on the desk. There were two drawers, and while both seemed empty, the size of the drawer didn't make sense. I tried to pry the bottom up, but it became clear that a latch was locking them in place.

I pulled both drawers out as far as they could and stared. There was obviously some mechanism that would open the hidden bottom. Past-me could have gotten this open in a second and I was sure that I could too. But the ache from my head was getting worse, and if the molly had got into my system, I was on a time limit.

It didn't take long for me to find a meat tenderizer in the kitchen. The first bottom took only four hits to break, while the second one took six. Out of one drawer, I found about five thousand dollars in cash and a folded piece of paper. Judging from the creases, it had been opened and closed time and time again. The only thing written on it was an address: *108 Rubboss Pl.*

But what caught my eye was the black leather pocket notebook that had been tucked away in the second drawer. I grabbed the book and began flipping through the pages:

Dsrov nb dlip szh yvvm tlrmt dvoo, r'ev mlgrxvw hlnv hgizmtv gsrmth drgs ghv xzkgzrm. Gsviv ziv hlnv gsrmth gszg gsvb zxxvkg zmw lgsvih gsvb yifh zhrwv. R wvxrwvw gl gzpv nzggvih rmgl nb ldm szmwh. Rg rh irhpb, yfg R zn tlrmt gl hgzig zmlgsvi fmwvixlevi lkvizgrlm. R droo yv tlrmt rmgl wiltfv zh z nzm mznvw Qzxly Sfmgvi. Gsrh mlgvyllp droo wlxfnvmg nb urmwrmth zmw, slkvufoob, hviev zh verwvmxv ru mvvwvw.

What the fuck was that?

"Of course, it's fucking encoded." I threw the stupid book on the ground. "I'll deal with this later."

I moved over to the bed and started removing the sheets. There weren't any cuts along the fabric, and the mattress was intact, too. But even as I was putting everything back into place, I couldn't help but feel like I was missing something. I checked again, but all I did was work myself up. I started to feel warm—really warm.

Logically, I knew that it was too soon for the molly to be affecting me, but that didn't mean I would risk it. I had no way of knowing if there was anything else laced with the drug, and while my last coffee had been decaf, 90 percent of what I'd consumed during the day had been caffeine. That, paired with my not remembering my own history with the stuff was enough to make me worried. Who knew how badly dehydrated or overheated I could get?

I took off my clothes and lay down on the floor. It felt like an overreaction, even as I was doing it, but it also seemed like my subconscious was looking for any excuse to get me to lie down and find what the bed had hidden. From my new position, the card taped to the underside of the box spring was obvious.

I ripped the thing off and stared. "You've got to be shitting me."

In my hand was another ID. The picture was of me, though my hair had been shorter and far better kept than it was now. There was only one other difference between the two cards: the names.

The first ID had listed me as Jacob Hunter. This ID was for an "Adam Campbell."

"Who the fuck am I?"

CHAPTER 5
CONSPIRACY UNVEILED

I'd spent the night in the house trying to gather my thoughts and waiting for a high that never actually came. In the morning, I put the different IDs in the wallet along with the cash and made my way to the streets.

While I was hesitant to order a ride, the combination of the distance and incredible heat would be a little too much for me to handle. I got dropped off a few streets away from Rubboss Place—a distance that would prevent anyone from knowing where I was going.

The walk over gave me a chance to understand a little more about the area. Instead of houses, the streets were full of warehouses and storage spaces. While most of the buildings looked abandoned, there were a few well-kept near where the road reached a dead-end.

When I finally reached the address, I was looking for, I found a large, nondescript, three-story warehouse. Gray paneling made up the walls and was only broken up by four red overhead garage doors and a small entryway along the north half of the building closest to the road. A quick scan of the place showed me that there were no windows.

I was only willing to get closer after I'd spent an hour outside and saw no one coming or going. I had to skip the front door; whether they had locked the door didn't matter when they had cameras set up. That left the garage doors. It would be a long and hard process to break those doors open—not to mention loud.

But it turned out I shouldn't have worried. I almost laughed when I saw the third door propped up at the bottom. It wasn't a big gap, but space under the couch hadn't been either. It took me scrapping my cheek and chest against the bottom of the door, but I'd managed to get through.

The room I found myself in was large and mostly concrete. A couple of forklifts lined one wall while unmarked crates covered the floor. Prying one open, I found it filled with black grains. Some of the grains had a yellowish substance coating their sides. I briefly considered trying some to try and identify it before I remembered the incident with the molly. Throwing them back into the container, I moved on.

The rest of the first floor was the same. Each room had containers that held either those black seeds or white crystals. When I exited the stairwell to the second floor, I found something a little more interesting. Though it had the same one-room layout, the crates had been replaced with countless computers. I went around to each one, but my persistence didn't help for once—though they had been kept on, each one of them required a password. Staring at them hadn't gotten me anywhere either; it seemed past-me wasn't good with computers.

I'd been about to give up and go to the third floor when the stairwell door opened. In a second, I had a gun drawn and ready. The young woman who had walked in threw her hands up in the air so fast that the green hair she'd tied up in a ponytail bounced. But her fear was gone in a second.

"Ah! Man! You scared me!"

If she knew me, this place was connected to Drogue. But something about the way she held herself convinced me she wasn't a threat. She was so happy and open. It seemed like she didn't know about the "orders" that the hooded man from the alley had mentioned.

Slowly, I lowered the gun but made sure that the safety was still released. I had to pick my words carefully. "Did you need something?"

"Oh, nah. Was just stuck with morning duty again. You know how it is."

"Sure."

"So... uh... what about you? Checking on the shipments?"

I glanced at the computers, so that's what they were for. But why did they need so many? And were the crates coming in or going out? If I could just log into one, I'd be able to find out.

I looked back at the woman; if she worked here, there was a setup here then she probably had an account. "Would you mind logging in for me? I seem to be having some... issues."

She laughed and started walking over. "Tech issues or 'old man' issues?"

I watched over her shoulder as she typed: *DrWhCOMP6-xlij7893*. With a small jingle, the lock screen faded away to a generic blue home screen.

"There we go, Mr. Boss-man!"

"Thank you."

"No problem. I get it—they keep changing the numbers at the end. If you need anything else, let me know. I'm right upstairs."

"I will. Have a good day."

"You too, Mr. Hunter!"

So, that was who she knew me as—Adam Campbell was still a mystery. But now wasn't the time to focus on that. I quickly pulled up the file folder and internet browser and began digging.

I focused on the history stored in the web browser first. It only went back a week, but it seemed to favor a mix of crypto websites and chat forms. Based on some of the posts, while this computer didn't have access to the dark web, it was being used often for management.

There wasn't a lot saved to the computer itself besides some spreadsheets. They seemed focused on the coming and going of materials in warehouse six. The purpose of this place seemed to switch every three months between housing raw materials, spare equipment, and drugs. Right now, it was dedicated to the materials needed for LSD and molly—the things I had found before.

I frowned. In the past, they had had a larger variety of materials, but the last six months, they had focused on gathering more hydrochloride salt and ergot.

"They've even started sending them to the same place..."

I shook my head. What the gang was doing shouldn't matter; I only needed to understand my ties to this. Then I hoped I'd find out why people wanted me dead. If the second floor would not help me with figuring that out, then there was only one other place left.

I knocked before opening the door at the top of the stairs. Inside was a smaller space that looked like it was meant for people to take breaks outside of a couple of offices. There was a mini fridge off to the side next to a TV. Across from it was an old leather couch in the room covered in different food wrappers. The woman from before was hovering over the sofa with a garbage bag, her eyes wide.

"You finished up a lot quicker than I thought you would... ha... ha..."

"Mind if I look around?"

"Of course not! You'll find that it's all spick-and-span! Just how you like it!"

I nodded to her before making my way toward the offices, only to be stopped by her grabbing my arm.

"Sorry, sorry, just... are you sure that Phil's okay with you going into his office all by yourself?"

I frowned. She had called me "boss" earlier and had been trying to keep the place up to my standards, so I'd assumed I must have some form of authority. But it wasn't enough, apparently.

I smiled, hoping that it was convincing. "He's fine with it."

I waited until she let go of me before rushing into the first office and locking the door behind me. I needed to act fast.

The office was standard: a desk with a computer and many filing cabinets decorating the place. The only thing that brought any life to the room was the small fake plant set up in the back. There weren't any windows to the outside, but there was one on the door, which meant that I at least needed to look calm.

I sat down behind the desk and tried the computer but quickly turned my attention to the drawers when the password from downstairs didn't work. There was mostly different office supplies stored inside, but I found myself rolling my eyes at the condoms. When I noticed that the woman wasn't paying attention, I moved over to the cabinets. There were several folders inside, some of which were just physical copies of the spreadsheets I'd seen on the computer. But others looked to be some form of sales records.

My eyes caught on the latest entries. A J. H. was listed near most of the newer sales. A sticky note had been attached to that part of the document: *Head for Dollys?*

As soon as I read the note, I was hit with an image of a teenage boy throwing up. When he'd finally stopped, he'd smiled so wide that his lips had cracked. His eyes had been glossed over, and he didn't understand what was happening as his body shook. I could remember nothing else, but I was sure that the boy was dead.

I looked back at the note. I didn't want to admit it, but J. H. was probably me.

There was a knocking sound at the door. Turning, I saw a man leaning against the door. His long, dirty-blond hair was put up in a bun. My stomach dropped as he waved.

"Still got my sweater, Hunt?"

CHAPTER 6
RACE AGAINST TIME

"Come on, Hunt. Let me in."

I took another look around the room. No exit would magically appear, but there might be something that I could use as leverage to talk my way out of the shit situation. The papers seemed important but considering the digital backups, threatening them wouldn't do much good. That meant I was down to my last option.

I leveled the gun, so it was visible from the door.

"Oh, come on—" The man shook his head. "We already played this game. And as the loser, I really don't feel like playing it again."

"Then what do you suggest?"

"A nice chat? It's been a while since I really got to stop and smell the roses, you know?" When I didn't lower the gun, the man sighed. A second later, the door slowly swung open to reveal that the man not only had a set of keys but also a revolver. "Did you think I didn't have the keys to my own office? Please. If I wanted you dead, you'd be dead. So, come on. Em cleaned up the place for you."

The man—Phil, if this was his office—had the upper hand; with no other option, I took a seat on the couch. "And where is 'Em?'"

"I told her we needed some... *privacy.* She ran off with her tail between her legs after that."

Instead of sitting next to me, Phil sat down on the table. His leg was bandaged, and he stretched it out to the side. He hadn't completely recovered from the shot, which meant that the gun was the only thing preventing me from running. Em was also a threat; she could be hidden anywhere in the building.

"What did you want to talk about?"

"Ah, ah, not so fast. We have to lay out the rules."

Phil waved the revolver in my face before pointing it upward and squeezing the trigger. I flinched, but instead of a bang, there was a click. With a smile, Phil spun the chamber.

My stomach turned. "Russian roulette?"

"Truth or shoot. If you can't answer or don't want to, you have to take a shot. The game will end when the gun's gone off six times or..." He let the sentence trail off and shrugged. "And the winner gets a brand new, slightly used car!"

I couldn't stop myself from letting out a small laugh at his game-show host voice. The entire thing was ridiculous. But I didn't have much of a choice.

"And if a person decides to lie?"

"We both know you're too good for that." He pushed the revolver into my free hand. "Alright, round one. What are you doing here?"

I looked down. I had both guns now. It would be easy to make an escape. But this was also a unique opportunity. Phil clearly knew me and Drogue. If he was willing to answer any questions I had, running might not be the smartest option. It helped that the game wasn't a threat if I always answered.

"I'm looking for information."

"About?"

I pushed the revolver back into his hands. "Pretty sure it's my turn to ask. So, what are we to one another?"

Phil's eyes widened. He looked even more shaken than when he realized there was a bullet in his knees. "You're really going for it, huh?"

He brought the gun to his temple. I moved to try and grab it, but he had pulled the trigger. The click was louder than anything I'd ever heard. He held out the revolver for me to take, but I couldn't move.

He'd almost died. He would die if we kept playing—and if not him, then me.

"We're done."

"That was only one of six, actually."

"Don't be fucking stupid."

"Worried about me?" Some of his confidence seemed back now. "Don't worry, the game's *perfectly* safe."

"You almost shot yourself in the head!"

He tried to push the gun into my hand, but I pulled away. When his second attempt to give me the gun didn't work, leveled it toward my forehead instead. "Are you forfeiting?"

"If I am?"

"Then I'll have to shoot all remaining shots right now." I went to take the gun from his hand, but he pulled it away. "New rule. I control the gun. So, ready to keep playing?"

I didn't know what to say. My mind raced, trying to figure out some way to get both of us out of this alive. But did I need to find a way? Realistically, playing until Phil lost would be the perfect scenario. I'd get answers, and my biggest threat would take itself out. It wasn't as if I wasn't a murderer. Yet—

The clicking of the gun startled me out of my thoughts.

"That's two of six." He turned the revolver around, so it faced himself. "I'll give you thirty seconds to ask your question."

Adrenaline pushed a question out of me before I could think. "What is 'Dollys?'"

"Shouldn't you know? It's that new mix we've got." The gun was pointed back at me. "Who is Dwight Duncan really?"

My stomach dropped. How could I answer that? "I don't know."

There was a long pause before Phil barked out a laugh. "Guess that's an acceptable answer. Your turn."

I needed to be smarter about this. I knew I was connected to drugs based on the supply I had back in the second place. Based on what he said, I was right to assume that J. H. mentioned in the files was me and that I was connected to Dollys in some way. But, at some point, the people in Drogue decided that I needed to be killed.

"Why is there a hit out on me?"

"Because that's what happens when we're faced with a traitor. Do you regret it?"

I wasn't sure what "it" was, though it probably concerned being labeled a traitor. However, I had no way of knowing if I *did* regret doing it or if that's what he wanted to hear. My eyes shifted to Phil's bandaged leg—if I couldn't answer about the betrayal, I could answer about that.

"I regret needing to hurt you." I waited for a second to see what Phil would do. When he turned the revolver back on himself, I took it as a sign that he'd accepted my answer and quickly spat out my next question. "Who is Adam Campbell?"

"No clue. Why didn't you kill me in the alleyway?"

The question surprised me. "I-I didn't need to."

Had I been the kind of person that he'd need to ask that? Though the three dots on my chest should have been enough to tell me that. If I killed them, then there would have been no reason for me not to have killed Phil, too.

I shook my head to try and clear it. It was my turn to ask a question. "Do you know who attacked me in my apartment?"

Phil laughed. "Don't tell me one of Cook's disguises actually paid off for once? Ah, we're never gonna get him out of that stupid uniform now."

I frowned to myself. The police officer from the parking lot hadn't been real. But, if that was who "Cook" was, then he couldn't have been who I was asking after. I pointed at my face. "I'm talking about who did this."

"If it were one of us, then you'd be dead."

So another party wanted me gone. At least the police wouldn't be able to charge me for attacking an officer.

Phil leaned forward and stared at me for a while. "Something is going on with you."

"That's not a question."

"Fair." Phil turned the gun back on himself, and a click echoed through the room. "Three of six. Your turn."

My mind was racing. What else did I need to know? "What's my address?"

"Why? Wanna know if we know about the place on Tral?"

I let out a small laugh and looked away. The apartment I had woken up in was on Filthments, and the one I'd stayed in last night was at Sweepage; there was another apartment I hadn't found yet, and it was probably infested with people looking to kill me.

Phil had just turned the gun back toward me to ask his next question when I heard the police sirens. I jumped up, panicked, but Phil seemed as casual as ever. "Hmm, sounds like your new car's almost here. Took them longer than I thought. Oh, come on. Don't give me that look! At least this way, there's a chance you'll live."

"They'll arrest you too."

"You really did forget shit then? Fuck... Guess I'll never really know. Alright." Phil pointed the gun up into the air and quickly fired off three shots—each causing the gun to click. "There. The game's officially done. Get out of here."

I only hesitated for a second before rushing toward the door. I'd almost made it when I felt something hard smack against my back. Turning around, I found a pair of keys, Phil's keys, on the ground.

"I parked around back. Take it. And don't say I never did anything for you."

CHAPTER 7
LOOMING DANGER

The black station wagon took a few tries to start and when it finally did, it showed that it only had a bit of gas left in it. I smacked the steering wheel. A part of me wanted to go back into the warehouse and shake Phil, but I knew that I didn't have the time for that. The sirens were getting louder.

There weren't many places to go unless I wanted to try and go off-roading. That meant that I'd have to go right past the patrol cars. The only advantage I had was that they weren't expecting me to be driving.

As I got onto the road, I could see them approaching; three vehicles had been dispatched. "What the hell did Phil say when he called them?"

I started down the road at the speed limit. I figured if I could seem like a normal person driving, then I might get past. I'd need to pull over when I got closer, but if I kept my head down, it would be fine. I'd only gotten a small way down the road when one of the patrol cars pulled out to the other lane.

When we were a little closer together, I drove over to the curb and let the car drift to a stop. The car that had gone into my lane began to turn to create a roadblock.

I cursed to myself. The calm approach would not work.

The patrol cars started to slow down, and I took my chance. Putting as much pressure onto the gas pedal as I could, I forced the steering wheel to turn as far to the right as it could. When my car started back up, it immediately jumped onto the curb.

While I made an arch around the car-turned-roadblock, I didn't manage fast enough. The front of his car smashed into my bumper, and I felt myself being wretched to the left.

I desperately turned the wheel. I had to regain control of the car. I fought against the rotation enough to prevent myself from turning completely around, but now I was heading straight toward one of the warehouses.

The smell of burnt rubber was trying to suffocate me. I kept pulling at the wheel.

By the time I angled the car back toward the road, the patrol cars had turned around. I barely got out ahead of them.

The entire car jolted as one of the officers hit the back of the car. Instead of stopping me or causing the car to spin out, the movement pushed my vehicle forward. I tried to think of what I could do. If I tried to turn, then the car behind me would just cause me to curve around. Stopping would do nothing, and I was already pushing the station wagon to go as fast as it could.

As much as I didn't like it, that left me with only one real option.

I turned my head to look; there was only one officer inside of the car. It took me a moment to free it from the back of my pants, but when I did, I turned off the safety and shot the gun toward the righthand side of the officer's vehicle.

The sound was amplified in the car, and, with my focus on driving, it was hard to handle the recoil. I was still more prepared for it than the officer. The pressure on the back of the car let up, slightly, and I blindly fired the gun again.

Through the rearview mirror, I could see one of the other patrol cars start to shift. It moved faster and with a curve that caused it to run into the car pushing me. The angle of it made both cars to splinter off in different directions. A second later, I felt my car started to be pulled. Being the last one in the chain, it was easy enough to fight against. The car behind me had a harder time—it only straightened out by going into the other lane.

It was the car that had started the splintering that had a problem. It was like the driver didn't even care to try and fight it. The car kept going at full speed right toward one of the buildings.

I ripped my eyes away from the mirror and focused on the road ahead of me. I heard nothing and prayed that it wasn't because my ears were still ringing from the shots; I did my best not to think about how I couldn't hear the sirens either. I needed to focus on getting out of the situation first.

The car in the lane next to mine turned, pushing into the body of mine. Looking over, I watched as the side mirrors of both cars were broken apart. Then I noticed the gun being aimed at me.

I ducked down. Shards of glass flew over from the right and lodged themselves into my side. There was a faint sting sensation, and I knew that it would hurt even more later when the adrenaline wore off—at least it wasn't a bullet.

Even with the road being a straight path, I knew I couldn't keep driving with my head down. Shooting at them wouldn't get me anywhere either; I wouldn't have time to aim a shot which means it would probably miss. If I managed to hit them, it would probably be lethal, and I'd end up killing *another* person.

I reached for the gearshift and forced it down to reverse. It took a second for the car to switch over, but when it did it let the patrol car pull ahead of me. As soon as it had cleared me, I threw the car back into drive and rammed into their bumper. They started to spin out, and I hurriedly drove past them.

A glance back a moment later told me that only one of the three cars was still in pursuit. The last officer was further back and seemingly unable to close the distance, but I knew that I was in trouble. The car was low on gas, and I'd be running on fumes soon. Thankfully, there was enough space between us that I saw the other car's tires if I fully turned.

I shifted around so that my foot stayed on the pedal as I sat backward in the seat. The officer seemed to have the same idea as me—only he wasn't aiming for a tire based on how he was holding the gun. I pulled the trigger, and it was only thanks to the recoil and flash I knew it had fired at all.

The officer's car veered off to the side. I'd done it. I turned back around and focused on the road. I wasn't in the clear, even if I wasn't being chased anymore. They knew the area I was in and what the car looked like. I just had a better chance now.

When I got about four blocks away, the car started to slow down. I pulled over and took a second to collect my breath. Then I noticed that the sleeves of my shirt felt wet. There was also a stinging sensation all over my right arm and at the top of my left one. I looked down and noticed all the blood.

I'd been expecting the glass stuck in my arm, but I hadn't noticed that I got shot. "Fuck."

I tried to turn on the car, but it didn't work. My heart was pounding. I felt like I was going to throw up. There wasn't an exit wound, so the bullet was still in my arm; I couldn't remember if that was good or not.

Either way, I had to get moving.

I pulled at the sleeve of my left arm, using the tear the bullet had made to rip it off. The effort caused more blood to appear on my right arm, and it hurt like a bitch. I wanted to scream. But finally, I got the fabric I needed. It was hard to wrap up the wound, and it wasn't as tight as it needed to be, but it was a start.

I got out of the car and began to make my way toward the apartment I'd woken up in when this all started. The Droguers knew about it, but I still needed to find somewhere to properly take care of myself.

One block later, I was completely winded. I needed to rest.

Another block, and I stumbled into an alleyway. I leaned back against the wall and slid down.

I was still too close. But if the police found me, then at least I'd get medical attention.

My eyes slid shut.

Maybe this was karma? The three dots weren't accurate anymore. There should be at least one more mark on my chest.

"Well, don't ya look like shit?"

I felt an arm wrap around my torso, but I couldn't get my eyes to open. All I could do was let the owner of the voice drag me away to wherever they wanted.

CHAPTER 8
UNSETTLING REVELATIONS

My mouth was dry. Every part of my body was in excruciating pain, but my mouth being dry stood out the most—probably because it was the one thing that felt something different. I waited for the typical hospital sounds to hit me, but they never came. All I heard were muffled voices and laughs.

When I finally opened my eyes, I found that I was in some bedroom. It wasn't a luxurious room, but the space had been carefully designed. The walls were painted red and matched the bedding, which was only a few shades darker. Cushions littered the floor, and the entire room was bathed in a soft light from the chandelier above the spacious bed.

While my right arm had been covered in bandages, only the upper part of my left one had been wrapped. There were also some bandages across my chest—probably to cover some other wound I couldn't remember.

It was a miracle that I was alive. I probably would have died if not for the person who dragged me away. Their voice had been familiar, but I couldn't place it. They clearly hadn't been police or a Droguer; I would have been in a hospital if it was the former, and had it been the latter, I wouldn't have woken up at all.

I forced myself out of bed and went through the one door in the room to find a hallway. Numbered doors lined the walls, and I realized I was in a hotel. I weighed my options before going toward the end of the hall with a beaded curtain. I'd only made it partway there when the curtain opened for a couple. The man was in plain clothing, while the woman who was leading him was dressed up in a skin-tight outfit.

When he saw me, the man laughed. "Someone likes it rough."

"Don't worry, I'll be nicer." The woman turned to shout back down the hall, "Edith's boy woke up!"

The pair continued past me but were quickly replaced by another woman. Her long black hair had been braided back, and that matched her black dress—something about her was familiar but I couldn't be sure. I had little time to think about it before she walked up to me and dragged me back down the corridor.

"Wait, I—"

"Hold yar horses. We can talk about it in our room."

I relented; as much as I hated to follow her lead, she was the one with the most knowledge about the situation. As soon as the door closed behind us, the woman, most likely Edith based on what the other woman had said, made toward the bed and laid down.

When she didn't speak right away, I took it as her way of letting me take the lead. "Why am I in a brothel?"

"That's the first question ya've got? Alright, well, couldn't have ya bleeding all over my apartment. 'Sides, I had to get ta work."

"So, you brought a man with a bullet wound here and did surgery on him?"

"Course not! We called in the doc, and she did it." She threw me a smile that was full of teeth and mischief. I glared back, half feeling like a parent scolding a child. When it was clear I would not back down, she sighed. "What was I supposed to do? Havin' a dead body down the street isn't exactly good for business. And the big boss would be pissed if the police came by and started digging inta everythin.'"

I felt my blood turn cold at the mention of a boss. I'd been stupid to let my guard down. A brothel would be tied to a gang. "You're a Droguer."

"What?" Edith sat up on the bed to gape at me. "Were ya listening to a word I said? I said we didn't want 'em here—not that they were our personal lap dog."

"The police and Drogue are..."

"Two peas-in-a-pod? Best'a friends? P-B-an'-J? Yeah."

I wanted to deny her claim, but it did make sense; Phil had pretty much admitted that he had nothing to worry about when it came to the police back in the warehouse. That meant that I was now tied up with another group.

I quickly scanned over Edith's body to try and find a clue as to who I was working with, but I couldn't find any. The action made Edith squirm. I quickly looked away. "Sorry."

"It's alright. Ya paying for the room anyways..."

"What?"

"Did ya think we'd let someone have a room for two nights free? Be glad the doc didn't send ya a bill!"

I rubbed my hand down my face only to wince at the pain that the action caused. Being out for two nights would explain why my muscles felt a little stiff, but it also meant that I had lost a lot of time. Not that that should matter; my identity wasn't going to disappear suddenly.

"Who am I indebted to?"

"No one. We already took the money from yar wallet."

I pushed down the urge to scream. "Then I guess I'll be going."

"Ah, come on, it's not that bad! We only took what we needed, honest! 'Sides I... sorta got you an appointment?"

"With who?"

"Dr. K. The therapist I told ya about."

I furrowed my brow, tuning the rest of what Edith was saying out so I could think. I had thought she was familiar, but the chances that the person who would have saved me was the same woman from Corners seemed slim. Still, if it was, that meant that I might have to deal with Dr. Katherine again; the thought alone made me want to run.

"I appreciate it, Edith, but—"

"Is it the vibe? She's got this 'knows all' vibe. I get that it's a bit creepy. But it's worth it! Everyone in Hogget goes to her!"

Was she a gang therapist, then? That would explain some of the unease I had felt—and why she seemed to know so much about how gangs worked. I suddenly felt stupid.

"Fine. I'll... give it another shot."

"Really? Ah man, that's awesome! Ya won't regret it! I promise!"

***

I leaned back into the same sofa from four days ago. The room hadn't changed at all save for a bit of dust that had tried to take over the place. Most of the scented candles had been lit but the weird combination of them made the room smell rotten.

Across from me, Dr. Katherine sat with her legs crossed. "I'm sorry that I made you uncomfortable before. Thank you for giving me another chance. Would you like to take the lead this time?"

"I don't know where I'd start."

"Well, what has happened over the past couple of days? Did you make any more discoveries about who Jacob Hunter is?"

I bit my lip. If she *were* connected to a gang, then she'd heard worse. She could also give me insight into some of the finer details I didn't remember. "I sold drugs. Dollys?"

"I... wasn't aware that that was on the street yet. Are you sure?"

I *wasn't* sure. Even when I had said it out loud, it had sounded wrong. But I had to be connected to the drugs. The information I had found in the warehouse had made that clear. There was also that stray memory of the boy dying—I'd seen that and mentally connected it to the drugs.

"I... killed people with it?"

"Oh, no, I don't think you need to worry about that. Just—"

My stomach turned, and a protest forced itself out of me. "No. No. It'll kill people." *It will kill people if I don't stop it.*

I moved to stand up and run out of the room only to find Dr. Katherine in front of me. She was pushing me back down.

"You need to breathe, Mr. Hunter."

But I couldn't.

How could I?

His blood was on my hands.

I let it happen.

I didn't remember how.

There'd be more blood on my hands if I didn't stop—

My head snapped to the side, and I felt myself start to settle back into my body. Dr. Katherine shook out her hand before taking her seat again.

"Now that we're a little calmer, Mr. Hunter, let's think. Is there anything else you know? About yourself or...about Dollys? Anything could help."

I thought back to the warehouse and the "game" I had played with Phil. "I'm a traitor? I've got this other ID. There's a Dwight Duncan..."

"What about places? Can you think of anywhere that might be... important to you?"

"There's some place on..." I trailed off before Tral could leave my lips.

"Yes?" Dr. Katherine was leaning forward now. "Please, Jacob, this is important. What if this is where they're making Dollys?"

It wasn't. I knew it wasn't. But she was looking at me expectantly, and I knew she would not let this go. "A place on Sweepage."

Her shoulders sagged, and she leaned back in her chair. "I see. Well, normally, I'd recommend going to see the place, but in this case, I'd recommend staying away. It could be dangerous."

"Right. Sorry, could we take a break? I'm feeling tired."

She smiled at me. "Of course. I can't imagine this is easy for you. Would you like something to drink?"

I looked over at the drink table. There was only tea. "No, it's alright. Just... need some air."

Before she could say anything else, I stood up and made my way to the door. I could hear her call out to me but chose to ignore it.

Instead of stopping in the lobby, I found myself outside the building. I hadn't spent a lot of time taking in the area before, but a glance around was all I needed to find exactly what I hoped for; a café was a little way down the street.

I made my way over. They had to have some coffee.

The inside was plain. Brick walls that had been painted white and fake plants were set up around the room. Though there were a lot of glass tables set up, nobody but the old man behind the counter was there.

When he looked up and saw me, the old man perked up. "Afternoon! Let me guess, a large black coffee with a spinach quiche?"

"That... sounds perfect, actually. Thank you."

"Any time." The man began working away behind the counter. I'd started to space out when he spoke again. "So, is Ms. Kokoro back, then?"

"Uh, sorry?"

"Ms. Kokoro. I haven't seen her around for a while. Or you, for that matter." The man started to laugh, oblivious to the whirlwind going through my mind. "Though, I guess it's a good thing when patients stop showing up? Though, she always says—"

I cut him off, finishing the sentence for him. "Everyone can benefit from talking to someone..."

A face flashed through my mind of a kind Japanese woman, her brown hair cut into a bob and a kind smile on her face as she encouraged me to open up.

I must have been standing there for too long because the old man spoke up again. "Officer Duncan? Are you alright?"

I looked up at the man, but that was all I could manage. My mind was too panicked. I had no idea who I had been speaking to, but it wasn't Dr. K. Law.

CHAPTER 9
ON THE RUN

For the thousandth time since I'd woken up with amnesia, I wished I had found my car in the apartment's parking lot. I was forced to walk to Tral Lane. While Drogue knew about the place, it was the only apartment I hadn't been to yet. It was also as just dangerous as the others, seeing as I'd told "Dr. Katherine" about Sweepage.

The walk was, theoretically, a good chance for me to clear my mind. But the more I thought about it, the more confused I became. I was Jacob Hunter, had an ID for Adam Campbell, and, based on what the man from the café had said, I was also a police officer named Duncan. Dollys were just as confusing, and trying to sort out the information was made worse by the fact that I had no idea if I could trust anything that Katherine had said.

All I could say for sure was that Dollys would end up killing many people. I had no evidence; the vague memories I had recalled were the only reason I could be sure that something happened. If the police and Drogue were connected, then my word wouldn't be enough anyways.

I could only hope that I would find something in the last apartment that could point me in the right direction. To do that, I needed to remember which building I'd lived in.

While I had originally planned on letting muscle memory lead me, the patrol cars outside of the one building made that unnecessary. It didn't look like anyone waited at the door. Going inside would be a risk, but I'd already accepted I'd having to do a lot of stupid things.

Keeping my head down, I hurried into the building. The lobby was small, containing only a set of mailboxes and an elevator with a buzzer next to it. While there was a door into the rest of the building, a quick tug showed that it was locked and needed a keycard.

I took out my wallet and looked through it, even though I knew there would be nothing useful inside. Sure enough, nothing had magically appeared and there weren't any hidden compartments I could have put the keycard in before I lost my memories.

But I had lived here and so that meant there was a chance someone would recognize me. I went over to the buzzer and started searching through the residents listed. The names weren't listed alphabetically, so they were probably listed based on room number. That made things a little easier for me; if I could find one of the three names, I knew then ringing the name next to mine would give me a neighbor.

After 20 clicks, I found a "D. Duncan" listed. I clicked one over and pressed the button to connect with "M. Vidal."

A few seconds later, a woman's voice with a heavily French accent picked up. "Allô?"

I searched my mind for any French I might know and put on an embarrassed voice. "Uh, bon-jer? This is Mr. Duncan. From next door? I, uh, locked myself out..."

I could make out the sound of someone muttering on the other side before a small red light turned on, on the side of the buzzer; a camera had been turned on. A second later, I heard a faint clicking sound from the door.

"Thank you!"

I ran over to the door and hurried in. While that had solved one problem, I still needed to figure out which room I lived in. There was no telling how many people of the 20 lived in the same apartment, which meant I could live in any of them. My best bet was trial and error.

"This is going to fucking suck."

***

After three failed attempts and one awkward conversation, I finally found the apartment of Dwight Duncan on the second floor. Of all the places that I supposedly owned; this was the first one that felt like an actual home. The couch and loveseat were the same brown color but the arms were a different design—one formed a sort of box around the cushions while the other one rounded and a part of the seat itself. Besides the sofas, there was a small TV, and a coffee table covered in coffee cups.

I moved to the sofas and began ripping them apart but found nothing. When a look around the room revealed no other hiding spots, I moved on to the next one. I skipped the kitchen, going toward what looked like an office, but a thorough search of the desk, chair, floor, and even walls came up with nothing. The bedroom was next to the office. It had a small bed placed under the window. I took off the orange bedding and lifted the mattress, but again, there was nothing. There wasn't anything else in the room to check: a bunch of puzzle books, running shoes, and a set of dumbbells.

It was after I had given up and gone to the bathroom to see if I could find any medical supplies that I found a clue about who I was. Hanging from the back of the door was a police uniform. It was too well made to be a fake.

That meant I was an officer who was a part of Drogue. But Phil had questioned who "Dwight Duncan" was. I must have approached one of the organizations with a fake name, or I could actually be Adam Campbell, and I'd given them both fake names.

I needed to sit down and think it all through. Unfortunately, I didn't get that chance. I had barely had the chance to lean against the sink when a loud knock emitted through the apartment. I stood frozen in place, my mind racing—it could just be Vidal from next door. But something told me I would not get so lucky.

As quietly as I could, I moved toward the front door and looked out the peephole. Two officers were waiting on the other side, their hands resting on their holsters. My eyes scanned around, but there wasn't any place to hide. There weren't any other doors out of the apartment, either.

How had they even known to come up to the room now? It couldn't have been that they watched me get into the building—too much time had passed for that. My mind jumped from possibility to possibility. Had someone reported a man trying to get into rooms then they wouldn't have needed to come here. Maybe someone had heard me searching? Or they had seen me through a window?

I took a deep breath. There was a window in the bedroom, and I was two stories up.

I'd only started to move when I heard another bang against the door. It differed from a knock; they were trying to kick the door down. I didn't care about being quiet anymore.

When I made it to the bedroom, a final loud bang sounded. I didn't need to turn around to know that they had made it inside—the pounding of feet on the ground was enough. From what I could hear, there was more than just the two I had seen.

The latch on the window was stuck. I could hear them getting closer, and for a second, I considered shooting out the glass. They'd be in the room any second.

I pushed harder. It moved up an inch then another and another. And finally, it was open enough for me to squeeze through.

I had wanted to lower myself down a little first to make it a little easier, but the door to the bedroom was ripped open. I didn't have time. I jumped.

The ground was getting closer, but I needed to stay calm. Before I hit the ground, I bent my knees. The balls of my feet impacted against the ground, and I could feel the force of it start to climb up my body. I needed to roll. As soon as my right forearm touched the ground, I could tell I made a mistake. There would not be any broken bones, but each cut that the broken car window had made on my arm screamed out.

"Freeze, Duncan!" I looked up to find an officer hanging out of the window I'd jumped from. Their large frame barely fit through the space. Still, their gun was pointed right at me.

I wouldn't be able to do anything without risking getting shot. I had made it through a lot in the last couple of days, but I doubted I could survive that—especially if this were an officer working with Drogue. I had no choice but to raise my hands in surrender.

The man ran a hand through his gelled-back blond hair. He glanced behind him and then jerked the gun. He was gesturing for me to leave. I squinted my eyes, trying to get a better view of him. Something seemed familiar. When I didn't move, the gesturing grew more frantic.

I couldn't understand why he would do this, but I didn't have time to think about it. If I had a chance to escape, then I needed to take it. With a small nod, I turned and ran. A part of me was still expecting to get shot, but I rounded the corner without a problem.

I kept running. It didn't take long for my exhaustion and injuries to catch up with me. I needed a place to rest and think. But if the police were waiting outside of this apartment, it was likely they were at the others as well, and I couldn't handle having to run away again.

There was only one place I could think of where I could avoid the police. It was far away, but I pushed forward. I was halfway through arranging for a room *without* a woman when I felt a hand smack gently against my back.

"Well, if it isn't my favorite not-customer." Edith beamed at me as she turned to lean against the counter before she went back to looking at her phone. "I was just thinkin' about ya? How'd things go with Dr. K?"

At the real name of the doctor, I felt myself relax. "I just need a place to stay for a few days."

"A few days? Oooh, didn't take ya for the ty—"

"That's not what I mean!" I yelled, causing her to tense up. "Fuck. Sorry. I just... had a long day."

"Well..." Edith smacked the counter. "Luckily, my shift's over."

I watched as the woman behind the counter handed Edith a sweater from behind the counter. A second later, she looked like she had when we first met at Corners. She had the same sweater covering the same dress and the same heels in her pocket—only the clutch bag was missing.

Suddenly, she was pulling at the back of my shirt. "Come on. Be any slower, and I'll leave ya here."

"Oh, no, Edith, you really don't have to—"

"I took in the stray cat, I gotta take care of him. Now, move. I wanna sleep."

CHAPTER 10
UNDERCOVER OPERATIONS

I ran my hand over the top of my head. It was strange not feeling any hair through my fingers, even though it had been a couple of days since I shaved it all off. But I knew it was necessary. I leaned forward, resting my elbows against my knees, and stared at the fuzzy, purple rug that took up most of the room. I hoped that it was as soft as it looked; Edith had been kind enough to take the floor while I stole her bed over the last couple of days.

Living in one room with a person that I barely knew had been somewhat suffocating. Edith had taken time off work to watch over me, claiming that she didn't want to come home to a dead body. I had appreciated it at first—besides the bed, there was only a small computer at a tiny desk with a beanbag for a chair in the room. Having another person to talk to gave me *something* to do. Two days into our living arrangements, though, she became overbearing. I understood that she didn't want me digging into her *things* or her private life, but her knocking at the bathroom door because I was "taking too long" grated my nerves. That was part of why I had sent her out with little requests.

Edith walked in through the front door with a bunch of clothes tucked under her arm, snapping me out of my trance. She threw them down on the bed before flopping down next to it. She scooped up one of the plushies—a polka dot dog—and held it to her chest.

"Ya really got a death wish, huh?"

I shook my head. "I doubt any of them will recognize me."

Approaching parts of a gang that wanted me dead *was* reckless. The only reason I was even considering it was my lack of options. All I had from "Jacob Hunter" were questions about Dollys, and well, Dwight Duncan had no presence online, only the fact that they were an officer. "Adam Campbell," meanwhile, was just as much a mystery as he had been when I first found the ID—it was looking like Campbell was someone I'd yet to live as.

And my identity wasn't the only problem anymore. I had no idea why Katherine had been interested in Dollys, but her questions had made me remember enough to know that it was dangerous. If there was a way to stop it, I needed to.

"Say what ya want, but if ya'r gonna risk ya life and still want me to research the fake doctor, ya need to pay upfront."

I pulled the wallet out of my back pocket and took out a few bills. When I put it back, I brushed a finger against the pocket notebook I had found. That was another thing I hadn't been able to find anything out about. I had hoped to find a key for the cipher at some point, but there hadn't been one. Unless I wanted to brute force it, it was almost useless.

I peeled myself off the bed and went to the clothes pile. There were many colors, materials, and sizes, but each one of them clearly came from a brothel. The thought of wearing any of them made me feel uncomfortable, but that drastic change in appearance was exactly what I needed. I took the clothes that would offer the most protection while covering up all the bandages: a brown leather jacket and a red long-sleeved shirt. The pants had a lot of zippers, but the only other option I had was to wear shorts.

I started to make my way out of the room when Edith spoke up, "Ya can just change in here."

I didn't bother responding to that. Instead, I made my way to the bathroom and quickly changed. I hurried back to find Edith was still on her bed, scrolling through her phone. Without the make-up or care put into her outfit, it was easy to tell just how young she was. It was also clear how under-fed she was.

Before putting my wallet and notebook back into one of the many pockets, I took out more money. "Here. Get us some dinner for when I get back."

"Ya really nice, Campbell. Maybe ya should forget Duncan and whoever else and stick with him."

I smiled as I made my way out of the apartment.

***

The little corner store that Edith had scouted out for me was on the other side of town from where I'd had my confrontation with Phil. A few people came and went and while most had paper bags, a few came out with cloth bags they hadn't gone in with. I watched their movements from the window, trying to memorize today's pattern.

When I was confident that I had it, I walked in. I could immediately feel the eyes of the man behind the cash register on me. Heading around to the back of the store, I circled the candy racks. Once, twice, three times around before going to the magazine stack across from the cash register. I scanned the different titles. From where I had been watching, I hadn't seen what they had been picking up. I'd hoped there would be one that was understocked, but that didn't seem to be the case.

There were all sorts of topics being covered: recipes, fashion, and even brochures of the city. My eyes lingered on the latter; a memory of picking one up and taking it to the counter itched at the back of my head. The first apartment had been full of brochures, too. Taking a deep breath, I picked one up and brought it to the counter.

"God, there's a lotta you today." The man reached under the counter and placed a cloth bag down.

"Phil wants your records."

I kept an easy smile on my face even as I held my breath. He stared at me for a beat before replacing the bag with a key. "The red binder."

"Thank you."

A minute later, I found myself back in Edith's car, driving down the street toward the next drop-off point that I'd scouted. It took me the rest of the afternoon, but I eventually got ten files from ten locations. As soon as it was done, I pulled up into a random plaza's parking lot and got to work.

From what I could tell, the fake doctor was at least honest with me about Dollys. None of the outposts were providing the new drug to sellers yet, but a few of the bigger places already had it. It seemed as if an issue caused a delay in the distribution. A few outposts that had been close to the apartment I had woken up in had stopped operating, causing the other ones to start selling more nine days before.

That meant that the change had happened two days before I lost my memories. That must have been when my "betrayal" was noticed or when they'd gotten everything they needed to catch me off guard. It didn't look like there was anything else that had happened around that time; there was nothing that would suggest someone else was involved. Yet, Phil was right when he said that if he or another Droguer had been the ones to find me, I'd be dead and not merely concussed. An officer, meanwhile, would have either killed me or had me arrested. But if nothing else had happened during the time then that third party wasn't an accomplice.

I smacked the edge of the steering wheel before throwing the last of the files back in the passenger seat. The entire thing was useless for figuring out anything about myself. And while I could hand it over to the police anonymously if they were as corrupt as some people had claimed, that still may not be enough to get everything shut down before Dollys were being sold.

I took out the notebook and looked it over again. It was my last clue, and it would only solve one of them. But, if there weren't any cipher, I'd need to find a pattern. I tried starting with the short words first, but after only 20 minutes, I threw the notebook to the side, too.

"At least I know I'm shit at that."

If I was terrible at solving codes, then past-me was probably bad at making them.

I turned the car on and started to make my way back to Edith's apartment. She wasn't home when I arrived, and while I felt bad for using her computer without her permission, I knew I would not figure this out on my own.

There was more to cryptography than I had expected. It took me a while to find any cipher that seemed simple, and that didn't require me to know what online encryption tool was used in the first place. Caesar ciphers involved shifting the alphabet over however many positions away. It didn't take long to find a website based around creating the cipher.

I put the first three words, "Dsrov nb dlip," into the textbox and began shifting the key. It didn't work. I needed to broaden my search. It took me using three websites to finally find something that made sense. The "atbash" code turned the mess into "while my work."

I just stared at the three words. I'd done it. A small laugh broke through me. "I did it."

"Did what?" I turned to find Edith standing at the front door with two greasy paper bags in her hands. She stood stiffly as she stared at the computer and notebook.

"Are you alright?"

"Yeah. 'Course. Ya find something?"

I held up the notebook for her to see before turning back to the computer to start inputting the rest of the paragraph. "A note from past me. I wrote it in atbash."

"Didn't mention ya had that... let me see." Before I could protest, Edith came up and tore the book out of my hand and replaced it with the bags she had. The smell of fries and bacon immediately hit me.

I opened up the bag and took out the burgers from the pile of fries that the bottom of the bag had become. The yellow paper wrapped around them had turned soggy from the grease. I tried to hand one of the burgers to Edith, but she was too focused on flipping through the pages of the notebook.

I tapped the burger against her stomach. "Did you find anything about Katherine?"

"Nah. No one knows what's up with her." She reached down and grabbed the burger and I frowned, noticing that one of her fake nails was missing. The ones that were still there were painted purple. "I think we just ended up stumbling on something random. Got nothing to do with yar 'amnesia."

I stared at her for a second. She kept the notebook, my one clue, tucked under her arm. I felt so stupid. One kind gesture and I had implicitly trusted her. And now I was in Edith's house, she had my only clue, and I had no idea when or why she had been in the apartment where I had lost my memories.

CHAPTER 11
BETRAYAL

I felt like I was walking on black ice, and any step I took could cause me to crash into the ground. The nail itself proved nothing. But she had given me the business card for Dr. K. Law. I had brushed that connection to the side and assumed that she had known the actual Dr. Law since she had used her actual name and because she was the reason I hadn't bled out in an alley.

But I didn't know why she would have tried to save me *or* insisted I go to therapy twice. It must connect with Dollys—that was what the fake therapist had been digging into. I also had no idea what would happen if she realized I had suspected her.

I took a bite out of my burger to seem normal. There were a lot of things on it: cheese, onions, bacon, and lettuce. I could taste none of it. It was just a heavy lump in my mouth that I had to force down. Across from me, Edith was eating her burger. She still had the notebook tucked under her arm.

I needed to get it back.

I still had the two guns. I'd kept them both close every day. But I didn't want to use them. There had been plenty of chances for Edith to have killed me; I didn't make sense to see her as a threat. I could wait until the middle of the night and escape while Edith was asleep, but that wouldn't give me any more information.

Edith was snapping her fingers in front of my face. "Ya good?"

"Yes. Sorry. I was just thinking."

"About?"

I licked my lips. "Everything."

"Well... well, I think ya should stop." She shifted so she was sitting on the ground, her back against the wall. "I mean, do ya really need to do all this diggin'? Can't ya just... start over? Become Adam or whatever and just live your life? Just leave!"

I laughed. She was right. From what I had found, past-me was probably a piece of shit. It would be easy to drop everything, move cities, and form a new identity or use "Adam Campbell."

But as easy as it was to fantasize about, it was also easy to see why it was impossible. "I need to know."

"Ya won't." Her voice was small, all the usual spunk and joy gone.

When I looked at her, there were tears on Edith's face. The burger was forgotten beside her and the book had been moved so she could clutch it to her chest. A part of me wanted to comfort her, but I noticed that her eyes weren't red.

"What about you?" I offered. "You could leave?"

"No, I owe her too much. I just..." The sound she made was a mix of a sob and a laugh. "Does it get easier? When they're not yar little stray?"

My mind flashed back to the police car that I had accidentally sent speeding toward the warehouse. There were three others, too, that I couldn't remember, burning at my chest. "No. It doesn't."

She hummed and stood up. Without thinking, I drew one of the guns and aimed it at her as she moved into the bathroom. I could hear her shuffling around, and then, a moment later, she was back. Instead of the notebook that she had gone in with, she had a small baton in hand. Along one edge of it, I could just make out a hint of reddish-brown.

A phantom pain ran through the side of my head. I tightened my grip on the gun. "Put it down, Edith."

"Or what? Ya'll shoot me? Thought it was hard for ya?" She stepped forward, her smile growing larger. "Or was that a lie to try and save yar guts?"

I licked my lips, my mind trying to frantically figure out how the image before me aligned with the young woman, the practical child, who had been so kind over the past couple of days.

"Last chance, *Adam*. Run off. Start fresh. Heck, I'm sure the boss will help ya if ya asked nice enough."

I kept my aim steady, and she seemed to take that as an answer. In a second, she was across the room with the baton raised above her head. It was only thanks to my instincts that I got my right arm up in time to block the blow. Pain rippled through the already hurt arm. I clenched my hand against the pain and felt a surge of panic run through me as I accidentally pulled the trigger. My body tensed as the bullet shot through the air and into the wall.

The recoil shook me, and before I could gather my bearings, Edith was on me again. She hit my left side in the exact spot where the bullet from the police chase had caught me. My vision turned white, and for a second, I thought I was going to throw up. I heard a clattering sound as the gun landed on the ground, and the next second I was being down with it.

Her foot started toward my neck, and I barely got my hands up in time to stop it. The entirety of my arms shook as I struggled. Eventually, though, I forced enough distance between my throat and her foot to push it to the right. With her off-balance, I rolled to the left and freed myself.

As I struggled into a crouching position, I noticed her foot coming for me. There was nothing I could except turn my head with the blow; the contact still hurt like hell, but it was better than a broken bone.

Before she could bring her foot back toward herself, I grabbed it and yanked with all my might. She clattered to the ground. When the impact hadn't been enough to make her drop the baton, I jumped on her arm.

Her free hand came up, and I could feel the fake nails digging into my shoulder. I bit my tongue and did my best to focus on getting the baton away rather than the pain; if I disarmed her, then the fight would be over, and we could finally *talk.*

With a firm hold on the baton, I twisted her wrist until she was forced to let it go. I threw it to the side and started to turn her around so her face would be against the ground. She allowed me to half-lift her before she reacted; her fist slammed into my crotch. My whole body tensed up, and I curled inward. A second punch and I was on the ground.

Edith shrugged my hand off her and started crawling across the floor. She wasn't going toward where I had thrown the baton, though. I followed the path that she was taking with my eyes, and my heart started to pound when I realized that she was going for the gun that I had dropped.

Pushing past the protests roaring through my body, I started after Edith. It took a few attempts, but eventually, I grabbed her ankle and started dragging her backward. Her free foot came up and started to flail around; I was too focused on getting hit I let my grip slacken enough for her to escape.

With one last lunge, she had the gun. We both hurried to stand. Edith turned as I reached behind my back to grab the second one.

There was a pause as we both stood, aiming at the other. She smiled at me. It wasn't like the smile she had thrown around the past few days—there was a crazed feeling to the joy that made her eyes shine. For a second, I could see her standing in the doorway of the apartment I had first woken up in.

I would never know why she let me live that night or if I was even meant to survive. There would be no talking her down. She was too determined.

She started to speak, but the sound of the gun drowned out her voice.

When I had fired blindly while I was in the alley with Phil, I had told myself that I had been sure that the shot wouldn't be fatal; the gun had been too low when I squeezed the trigger to actually kill.

When I had fired in the car, I wasn't sure what had happened. Without seeing it, I could lie to myself about what had happened.

When I looked at the three dots on my chest, I could feel the weight of the action, but it was abstract. I didn't remember it and didn't really *know* what I had done.

But as I looked at Edith, her body splayed across the floor from the force of the bullet that had lodged itself inside of her forehead; there was no avoiding what I had done. Blood and little flecks of *something* were pooling around her head. The red stood out against the black of her hair.

That warped smile was still on her face. She hadn't thought I would shoot. I couldn't blame her—I would not either.

I stepped over her and made my way into the bathroom. The black notebook was set up on the sink. My body had shaken by the time I made it back into the main room. When I took a deep breath to try and steady myself, all I could smell was copper. My body started to shake even more.

It was a little difficult to dislodge the blanket from the bed, but I managed it with only one of the stuffed animals, the stupid polka-dot bear, falling to the ground. I considered it for a moment before picking it up and walking back to Edith.

I closed her eyes, replaced the gun with the bear, and covered her with the blanket.

Taking the car keys with me, I walked out of the apartment building and outside. It was a nice day, though kind of cold.

It took a while to get to the alleyway, but as soon as I was there, I started to throw up. My legs were shaking too hard to keep me standing. I barely noticed the impact on my knees as my stomach lurched again. A sob tore through me.

Alone in the alleyway, I let myself break down.

CHAPTER 12
IN PURSUIT OF ANSWERS

I sat in the car and stared at the "therapist's" building. Katherine had been connected to this in some way. The notebook was in the seat next to me. Every time I had tried to think about where I could go to decode it, Edith's face—the one that had looked so young and joyful—would flash in my head. It was stupid, but I couldn't face it yet.

I refocused on the building. There had been no signs that there was anyone inside while I was waiting. It made sense that the place would be deserted; there weren't a lot of situations where you'd need a fake therapist.

Apparently, you only did that when you needed to dig around in an amnesiac's head.

Even if they had fled, though, I was sure that I could find some form of clue inside. At the very least, maybe Dr. Kokoro's actual notes were inside. Maybe I could remember more about myself if I read the notes from when the two of us met up.

I opened the car door and strolled over to the front door. It wasn't locked, letting me just walk right in. The small desk for the receptionist was empty. The drawers had been emptied, and the only thing on top of it was the phone and computer. I tried both, only to find they had been disconnected. I looked down under the desk but couldn't make sense of the mess of wires I was met with.

Deciding I could come back to it later, I moved over to the main office where the sessions had been held. The layer of dust had gotten worse, as had the smell that I'd noticed when I sat down for my second appointment. If I hadn't already thrown up, I'd probably be sick again.

I kept the door open as I began searching through the filing cabinet next to the door. The entire thing was filled with folders that had been marked with a name and sorted out alphabetically. It didn't take long to find "Duncan, Dwight" in the midst.

The folder was thin with only a few papers inside of it. One sheet was mostly blank, save a few words written in the same messy scrawl that had been in the black notebook. The paper made little sense; the words were randomly written around the page and ranged from things like "night" to "crying."

The other pages inside the folder were typed and seemed to provide a reflection on Dr. Kokoro's thought process during our appointments. I looked over the page with a one drawn in the corner.

During the hour, Dwight displayed a reluctance to discuss the issues that he had been recommended to me for. When I brought up the first exercise, he became agitated and began pacing the room. Further probing only worsened Dwight's condition.

More sessions than originally anticipated may be needed. I shall be recommending that Dwight be given four months' leave to prevent any incidents or harm from occurring. If no signs of improvement have occurred it may be beneficial for him to be taken off of the force.

My hands felt heavy as I read over the report again. My mind supplied me with the memory of pacing around a circular table in this room and feeling frustrated. But, as hard as I tried, I couldn't remember *why* I had come to Dr. Kokoro . Based on the report, I hadn't come here willingly; it seemed to have something to do with my job as an officer.

The other three pages covered the other sessions. I had displayed signs of aggression and frustration whenever we had gotten closer to discussing "the main incident." Dr. Kokoro had, apparently, been unable to even start me on the first step and had taken to labeling me as incredibly avoidant.

I folded up the pages and looked around the rest of the room. My eyes landed on the table; it wasn't the same as the one from the memory I'd recovered. Walking toward it, the smell was getting worse. I gagged as I stood over the table.

The smell was coming from inside of the wood.

It took a while, but I eventually found a small seam along the bottom of the oak cube. Someone had turned the table upside down to hide the fact that it could be opened. Because of the design, there had been no sign that it had been placed incorrectly—I likely still wouldn't have if not because I was specifically looking.

I pushed the box over. While the base fell over, the lid stayed on the ground. From the space that I had opened, a ton of plastic rolled out. How the sheet had been layered made it hard to see through it. The smell was a big part of the reason I even guessed what it was.

The reddish sludge and indent made it hard to make out her face but it wasn't hard to guess that this had to have been the real Dr. Kokoro Law. Her body had started to bloat, and the green hue of her flesh was turning red—probably dead for six to nine days. It had been eight days since I woke up with amnesia.

"Fuck." I whispered to myself and started to pace the room. "Fuck. Fuck!"

It hit me how big this was. I had known that she was probably dead, but I hadn't imagined that I'd sat in front of the fucking body and hadn't fucking noticed. I had barely even questioned the smell.

And now my fingerprints were all over the scene. I could try and clean them off, but then I would risk getting rid of any evidence that pointed to the actual culprit. I tried to take a steadying breath, but the smell had gotten ten times worse now that the body had been uncovered.

I hurried out of the building—I couldn't fucking handle it.

***

The cheap chair in the library felt like a luxury after sleeping in the cramped car. I set the notebook down beside me as I started up the computer. There were two things I needed to do: one was to properly decode the book, and the second was to look at the news.

After agonizing over it, I called in an anonymous tip about Dr. Kokoro. I didn't have the resources to uncover what had happened to her on my own. The only option I had was to turn it over to the police; if they tried to cover it up, I would know that it was Drogue, and if they didn't, then they might do their job.

There was also the code. As sick as what I'd done to get the book back made it, I had to face it. I didn't have time to be "*avoidant.*"

The homepage of the computer's web browser was the local news site. It didn't take long to find the article I was hoping for: "Therapist Body Found at Office—Gang Involvement Suspected."

I quickly read through the article. The details were sparse but covered what I expected. It noted that there was an anonymous tip that the police had arrived at the scene and confirmed someone had died. The part that shocked me was when the journalist seemed to go off script and decided to add their speculations. It was in their rambling theories I saw the name "Hogget." I didn't need to read the author's words to know what it was.

Splashes of memories jumped in my head. A large, classy apartment spoke to the boss's wealth, and the hoard of people lined up to take orders was a clear sign of his power. I'd been too old to be considered a "commodity"—thank fuck—and was given the job of a cage fighter and, later, a bodyguard to the boss himself. I stood around for years, watching and fighting and getting praised for the hoard of people I'd taken out to protect him.

"Now, this is the kind of man my daughter should've married!"

My heart started to race, and I took a deep breath to try to calm myself down. I'd finally found out the Adam Campbell identity; I'd been the loyal lapdog to the boss of one of the central gangs in the city.

I laughed. "Fuck me. Past-me probably couldn't even keep up with half this shit."

While I wanted to sit with the new revelation for a while, I had other things I needed to do. I quickly made my way back to the website that I had found in Edith's apartment and started typing. It didn't take long, and soon, I was staring at the message:

While my work has been going well, I've noticed strange things with the captain. There are things that they accept and others they brush aside. I took matters into my own hands. It is risky, but I will start another undercover operation. I will go into Drogue as a man named Jacob Hunter. This notebook will document my findings and, I hope, serve as evidence if needed.

While I had a vague memory of writing it and desperately trying to encode it, I couldn't remember much else. It mentioned starting *another* operation, but which identity was the fake one that I'd taken on? Who was the captain?

There was one way I might find answers. I turned the page and began typing in the rest of my entries.

CHAPTER 13
UNRAVELING CONNECTIONS

It had taken most of the day, but I'd finally finished decoding the rest of the messages. If there was one thing I had learned, it was that I was a shit writer. It was more common than not for an entry to just end abruptly. What must have made sense at the time of writing was useless without the context needed to understand it. The few memories that the entries did reveal were centered on working with Phil to ensure shipments of drugs and the materials needed to create them. I hadn't been selling them, like I thought, but been organizing the creation of them.

That meant that I, as Jacob Hunter, had wriggled my way far into Drogue's operations and learned where most warehouses were located. They had all been noted down on the fifth page of the notebook with a number and a four-digit code. Based on the different colors of ink, I kept returning to this page to add the information as I learned it.

The newest location, number three, had a note next to it—it was where the "new" stock was being created. From everything I learned, that new stock would be Dolly's. There was no sign of the danger that Dollys had or even a note about how they were made. I had stopped writing after I'd been sent to work on the new project.

My goal had been to take this information to Hogget as Adam Campbell or to the police as Dwight Duncan. While I had no idea what Hogget would do with the information, I knew that the police would burn the notebook.

With a deep breath, I turned off the computer and stood up. It was a long track toward the car despite the short distance.

I had killed someone for this information.

It was at least going to do some good.

***

The warehouse listed as the place where Dollys was created was a two-hour drive from the city with the stop I needed to make. As I got closer, I realized that it was a factory. Three chimneys towered over the place, though none had any smoke. Parts of the wall near the top of the building were a slightly different color, hinting at the building's age, but the rest of the lot seemed brand new. Even the grass that surrounded the road and parking lot was meticulously maintained.

Several cars were littered around the lot, including a few unmarked delivery trucks. Some people were running from place to place, trying to manage everything, while others were sitting around, smoking or drinking. It took a while, but I finally found a fairly isolated spot.

It wasn't clear whether Dollys were being produced here; three months may have passed since I wrote the address down in my notebook. But, even if it wasn't, this pace was important to their operations. I recited the code from the notebook in my head as I got out of my car with my duffle bag and started to make my way to the main door.

I felt a few eyes on me as I walked, but I kept going, and no one stopped me. The code—0264—was accepted; that it hadn't been changed since I was marked a "traitor" surprised me, but I could let no one see that. I needed to look calm and in control, especially if someone was watching the camera pointed at the door.

I made my way inside and quickly scanned the area. Despite how busy the place had seemed, no one was on this floor. The ceiling was raised, making room for the different conveyor belts and machines lined up across the floor. Dust, boxes, and wooden creates covered every surface. I hurried over to one of the boxes and opened the lid. Instead of the black seeds or white crystals, I found several circular containers labeled with an "M" and filled with a white powder—it must have been molly.

I took out one of the containers and popped off the lid. I took the tiniest bit from the container and placed it on the tip of my tongue, only to immediately spit it out. It was nothing like what I had experienced when I tried it in the apartment; this powder *burned.* I put the container back inside the box and hurried further into the building.

There was a door set up underneath a metal staircase in the back of the room. I peeked through the door to find what looked like a loading zone. People hurried back and forth, some carrying boxes in and others carrying boxes out. If I knew no better, it would seem like this was any *legal* shipping business.

Deciding this room wouldn't work either, I closed the door and made my way up the stairs. My footsteps echoed around the room with each step. While I did my best to keep an air of confidence, my eyes kept darting between the door at the top of the stairs and the one below—looking for any sign of a person coming to check walking around. Luckily, I made it up without incident.

The second floor comprised a larger hallway with different rooms. A peek inside a few showed that they were labs with only a small bathroom set up near the back. At least one person was inside each lab where they were mixing two white powders from circular containers like the one I found on the first floor. I knew that it would be just as dangerous to start the plan there as it was downstairs, but I could feel my nerves starting to get the best of me.

I took the duffle bag from my shoulder and pulled out the plastic bag I had set up on the ride over. The different novelty shirts had absorbed most of the vodka. I placed the shirts in a line along the middle of the hallway, careful to make sure that each touched the other. When it was ready, I took out the lighter.

The sharp, alcoholic smell that had taken over the hallway was quickly replaced with smoke. It didn't take long for the flames to spread down the path I had made.

I hurried toward the bathroom and took a deep breath, "FIRE! FIRE!"

I opened the door, slipped the lighter into my pocket, and hid. The sirens started up and panic took over.

CHAPTER 14
SHOWDOWN

When the panicked footsteps had finally faded, I slipped out of the bathroom and used the water bottles I had packed to put out the flames. I had a lot that I needed to do before I let the place burn down.

While it was easy to break each of the different pieces of lab equipment, the sheer number of things made it take longer than I had wanted. My focus was to make sure that the different containers—the one labeled "M" and the other labeled "L"—were emptied down the sink and washed away. Even if this didn't fully stop production, this much-lost product would cause problems. As I worked, I kept an eye out for any papers that might better show me how the operation worked, but all I could find were strings of formulas I couldn't understand.

I was almost done with the final lab when I heard metal being hit in a steady beat. I hadn't worked fast enough. I still needed to destroy the product that was downstairs, but I doubted that the person coming up would allow that.

Taking my gun out from behind my back, I slung the duffle bag over my shoulder and crept into the hallway. I shot when the door started to open. The drywall shattered and the door was wrenched closed by the person who had been approaching.

A familiar voice called out, "Is this your new greeting or something?"

I ignored Phil's teasing—I needed to stay calm. There were no other exits on this floor, which meant that I needed to either find some way to slip past him or fight. Even if I got out of this one unscathed, how many people would be waiting for me outside?

"I'm just gonna—" the rest of his sentence was cut off by the gunshot—"Oh-kay! Or not."

I needed to buy myself some time to think. "What you're doing here is sick! These drugs are... you're sick!"

"Says the man who came up with Dollys!"

My stomach dropped. Was that why I had felt so responsible? Vaguely, I could remember Phil pulling me into a side hug, alcohol on his breath as he celebrated for me. But I didn't know chemistry—I didn't understand a single one of the formulas I had found.

"You're lying."

"That another part of your memory you lost? Come on, Hunt, think about it. All those hours slaving away at those textbooks gotta be somewhere in there." My stomach twisted.

Phil took my silence as a sign to continue. "Listen. I'm not armed. Just wanna come talk."

The door started to open again, but I couldn't find it in me to fire. Soon, Phil was walking up to me. The cast on his leg had been removed, but he was still limping. As he got closer, I realized that his hands were behind his back.

"Freeze. Hands up!"

"Still don't trust me, huh?" He brought his hands out and aimed the revolver toward me. "Smart."

"Drop it."

"It wasn't loaded last time."

"I don't give a fuck. Drop it."

"Fine. Fine." He pointed the gun toward the ceiling and started to crouch down.

As he shifted, I noticed a hint of movement on the stairs. I had assumed he was alone because I had heard nothing —I was wrong. I jumped into the door of the lab I had been in. A gunshot rang through the air.

"I told you to wait!" Phil yelled.

Whoever else was here no longer cared for stealth. I could hear two sets of footsteps hurrying toward me. I didn't look back as I closed and locked the door. That wouldn't hold them; I needed to think.

There was an island at the center of the room and several cabinets attached to the wall. The room was windowless, but if they were making drugs in here, they'd have needed some ventilation. Scanning the ceiling, I found a vent. It was a little ways away from the island but easy enough to reach.

My arms shook as I tried to pull myself up, but I managed. It was too tight a fit to turn and close the vent behind me. They'd know where I went, which meant I needed to be fast. While the air duct would lead outside, roughly three stories up would be too high to jump down. I needed to get out in one of the other labs.

As I was lowering myself down in the next lab over, I heard a gun fire and then a door being kicked open. Now was my chance to run. I hurried into the hall and onto the stairs, where I knew I had made a mistake. The sound of my foot against the metal rang out in the otherwise silent space.

"Shit."

There was no going back now. I took it two steps at a time, looking over my shoulder constantly. As soon as I saw the door open, I raised the gun and fired. There was a scream as the bullet hit one of them—non-fatally, hopefully. Even with one down, there were still two others to worry about.

My footsteps were soon joined by another pair on the stairs. I looked back to see Phil hurrying after me while a woman stood in the doorway over another person. She had her gun aimed toward me. I crouched down, trying to make myself smaller. Her shot went wide.

I had turned to fire back only to find Phil jumping. He flew through the sky toward me, and the force sent the both of us down. I could feel the impact, first on my shoulder, then my hand, my back, my elbow, and my knee. At some point,

Phil's body and my body detangled, and I could catch glimpses of him ahead of me as he fell faster. The gun was no longer in my hand. The duffle bag, which had taken a lot of the impact, was wet; one of the alcohol bottles inside had broken.

My body protested as I rolled over. The duffle bag was left behind at the base of the stairs. I hope it was soaked enough it would be a good distraction. I took out the lighter, flicked it on, and threw it at the duffle bag.

While it didn't explode, the fire was a lot worse than I had anticipated. It was enough to prevent the woman from coming down after me. Darting under the stairs, I was out of her point of view.

The only threat left was Phil. I looked back. He was still laid out on the floor and while he had rolled his head to look at me, he made no sign of moving.

I opened the door to the loading zone and ran.

CHAPTER 15
RECKONING

The people outside were disorganized and easy to slip past. I watched the road as I made my way over to the car. No one was leaving the lot. With a two-hour stretch of empty road, one gun, and countless people around, I knew there was no way I could sneak away. I slipped into the back seat, positioned myself so I wouldn't be seen with a glance, and waited.

It was hard to hear what was happening around me, but that was the only choice I had. If I got caught, then I'd never be able to finish what I started. I sat curled up for so long that my legs started to ache. I was considering looking when I heard the sirens getting closer. A while later, red and blue lights started to dance on the roof of the car. It could have been a fire truck, but I doubted it.

There weren't a lot of options for me. All I could do was stay still and hope that everyone left soon.

I had almost fallen asleep when suddenly the driver's door opened. I reached for my second gun—my only gun now— when the door closed.

"You can shoot me if you want, but then you're really not getting out of here," Phil said. "Now, give me the keys."

I threw the keys toward him. "How did you know I was here?"

"It was the only one over here." The car started up, and Phil had pulled out of the lot. "Not your best plan."

He kept driving, and I kept my hand on the gun. "Where are you taking us?"

"*I'm* going to get the fuck out of town before they decided to finally pull the trigger. *You* can get out wherever you want."

I sat up and looked back at the factory. Two police cars were set around the building and a handful of uniformed officers were mixed in with the Droguers. They were all looking around—looking for me.

It would be easy to go with Phil. I'd already disrupted part of the Dollys operation and had done all that I could to figure out who I was. I could start over, like Edith had suggested. But I couldn't then, and I couldn't now.

"Drop me off in town."

"Anywhere specific?"

I shook my head. "I don't know? The library?"

"Do you not have anywhere to stay?" He glanced at me out of the corner of his eyes. "Fuck... you're an idiot."

***

Phil pulled up beside an apartment and parked. As I opened the car door, I felt something smack against my shoulder with a *clang*. I turned and found a P.A. keyring on the seat beside me. There had to be 20 keys there.

"You're gonna need those to get in. The codes eight, nine, zero, one." He smiled. "Good luck figuring out which one opens the door."

I took the keys and weighed them in my hand. Soon, he'd drive off and I'd lose the chance to ask the one question that had been burning in my mind almost the entire drive.

"Did I... did I really invent Dollys?"

"Sort of? You're the one who pushed mixing molly and LSD. Said we could market it as a fun new party drug."

"Not a poison?"

He let out a small laugh. "We'd both be dead if it was."

"Someone died—" I ran my hand along the top of my head—"and you're laughing."

"No one died!"

"He did! I-I saw it. I... remember it."

Phil tapped the back of his head against the seat a couple of times. "God, no wonder you were being so stupid about this... I didn't know. I swear, I didn't..."

I stared at the keys in my hand. When I moved my arm away, Phil didn't fight it. "Goodbye."

The car door slammed behind me. I hurried into the building, put in the code, and walked toward the elevator. As I looked at the call button, I realized I had no idea which unit was under Phil's name.

Looking over my shoulder, I saw the car starting to drive off. I tried to fight off a small smile. "Asshole."

***

I hurried inside when I realized that the key worked. The apartment was a bachelor pad, with a small bathroom. The sofa was a gray pull-out that had been covered in different throw blankets, most of which had some strange stain on it. A bunch of pillows were on the floor and around the little table where a tiny TV had been set up. The makeshift kitchen Phil had set up was a lot like the one I had found in the first apartment: a fold-out table, microwave, and fridge. There was also a small electric kettle—probably used to make all the instant noodles cups that were around the place.

My stomach had turned from the smell of mildew and old food, but it had been a long time since I ate. I needed something. It took a while, but I scavenged a beef jerky pack from the back of the fridge. It was cold and tough, but at least I knew it wasn't rotten.

After eating, I did another search of the place to see if I could find any cleaning supplies. The only thing that Phil had were garbage bags. I shuddered but got to work, the mindless task keeping my hands busy as I reflected on everything.

I needed a new plan—one better thought out. The only reason I had made it out of the warehouse was because of luck and whatever past relationship I had with Phil. Going back to the source now with no sort of backup would only end up with me dead in some unmarked grave and Dollys all over the street.

The only good thing was that there'd been far less police than I had expected. It was possible that they weren't as controlled by Drogue as I thought, but I still wasn't willing to hand everything over to them. I had no physical evidence, and it would take only one corrupt officer to sneak someone into holding and have me killed. There was also a chance that I'd be thrown in jail, and somehow that seemed even worse. God only knew what the fuck a bunch of inmates would do with someone who was labeled a "traitor" to Drogue.

That left me with one of two options: I could either disrupt the distribution or let people know what was going on. The first option was as risky as going after the source, but creating mass hysteria could backfire. There was also the fact that the second plan required people to pay attention; if I stood in the city screaming warnings, I'd just be labeled as crazy. Going online wouldn't work either. There were at least a million posts uploaded to the internet every day and I didn't understand technology enough to know how to get people looking at whatever statement I made.

I also had to figure out why what I understood about Dollys didn't match with what Phil had told me.

I closed my eyes and lay down on the pullout. Every muscle in my body was sore. There was still a lot that needed to be done, but I decided to let myself rest. I'd already made a massive dent in the operation. I had time.

CHAPTER 16
DRAMATIC ESCALATION

"Three more people have been found dead—"

I turned off the TV, barely resisting the temptation to throw the remote at the screen. It had been only three days, but seven people had died from a "mysterious illness." I wanted to believe that it had nothing to do with Dollys, but the list of symptoms that people were being warned about matched up perfectly with my memory of the young boy dying.

I had clearly underestimated how far along their production was—or how quickly they could react. As long as there was a way for them to get Dollys out to people, the Droguers would.

Without a car, I was back to walking, and Phil's apartment was positioned so it was nowhere near a convenience store. It was mid-afternoon by the time I found the shop—right around when their reports suggested that the next wave of sellers would come for supplies. But if I were to sit in the parking lot, staring into the window, then there was no way they wouldn't catch on.

I stumbled into the store with my head down. It didn't take long to grab a pack of beers from the back and stagger back toward the counter.

I slammed down some cash, along with the beer and a lighter. When I spoke, I made sure I slurred my words, "And a smoke."

My heart wouldn't stop pounding, and I could barely breathe as I waited. It had only been a few days since I was last here; all it took was for this man to look closely at me for this plan to fall through. The money was dragged across the floor and, a moment later, was replaced with a pack of cigarettes.

I scoped everything up and started to make my way to the door. "Hey! Buddy!"

Shit "Huh?"

"You forgot your change."

"Oh..." I felt my shoulders drop. I was relieved, but that didn't mean I could turn around and go back to risk it again. "Keep it."

The door slammed shut behind me, and I made my way to the other side of the parking lot. It only took a moment to make myself look like some random drunk guy no one wanted to look at. The asphalt was freezing, and between dealing with the cold, acting drunk, and pretending to be smoking, I was fucking miserable.

It took half an hour, but eventually, I caught someone circling the back of the store, going to the movie rack, and then to the counter. The man was wearing a large gray hoodie and a matching pair of sweatpants which clashed with the cloth bag he had been given. His hood was pulled up, hiding his face.

I pushed myself up, still pretending to be drunk, and began to follow the man. The gun felt heavy against my back as I walked. I didn't want to use it again, but if I already had blood on my hand—if past-me had been a serial killer—what was another death?

I could do it.

As soon as the man reached an alleyway, I rushed forward and placed the gun at the back of his head. My hands were shaking. "Hand it over."

"We cool." The man's voice was shaking. "We cool."

"Hand. It. Over."

"Yeah, yeah, you got it, man."

As soon as the bag hit the ground, I grabbed it and threw it over my shoulder. With my attention elsewhere, the man took his chance to wheel around and punch me in the face. I stumbled back but would keep my grip on the bag.

But it wasn't the bag that the man was going for. He easily ripped the gun away from me. The barrel was barely touching my forehead, but it felt so heavy. I forced myself to stop thinking and to just *move*.

I bent my knees and lunged. My arms wrapped around his stomach and pushed. We both hit the ground. I pulled back enough to punch him—once, twice, three times—in the face.

The man brought up his arms to block me, and I finally realized that he wasn't holding the gun anymore.

Quickly looking around the alley, I saw it behind us. With one last punch to the man's gut, I crawled my way over to it. I was sure to keep my distance when I turned around and pointed the gun at him. The man froze mid-squat and stared at me.

"You're going to tell all your friends that Drogue doesn't sell drugs anymore, okay?"

The man laughed. "Might as well shoot me, bud."

My hands shook. It would help get the message across. I closed my eyes and stepped forward.

The man let out a groan as the butt of the gun smashed against the top of his head. I opened my eyes to see him curled up on the ground. Blood was running down his forehead, but it was easy to see that he was still breathing.

I turned around and started toward a pawn shop—threats wouldn't work, but that didn't mean I couldn't try a different angle.

***

I sat on the sofa in the apartment, my new phone in hand, and stared at the new audio file. I clicked on it for a third time in a row.

The first voice was my own. "Who's your supplier?"

"L-Leo Campo," the young lady had replied. She'd been shaking, tears running down her face. There was a bit of blood along the edge of her afro from when I hit her. But the recorder was for audio—no one else would know about it except for me and her.

"And who gives to Leo?"

"Drogue."

"And what drugs are you selling?"

"Uh, m-molly. LSD. Uhh..."

"Heard of 'Dollys?'"

"Y-yeah. That's the- the new stuff."

"Is it dangerous?" I had asked while nodding my head.

"Y-yes?"

The audio file cut off there. I'd let the woman run away. She had been so fucking scared.

I hit the play button again—let the words fill the room again. That had been the fourth dealer that I'd cornered. The second and third ones had both noticed that I was tailing them. While the second one had decided to outrun me, the third had decided to fight. My muscles ached at the memory. I'd been lucky that the woman had decided to "take pity on the junkie." But it had made me angry and reckless; the terror in the recording made it clear I'd gone too far.

I felt sick as I wondered if past-me had done things like this, too. I shook my head; it didn't matter anymore. I'd done them, and now I had something tangible that I could use against Drogue.

But I wouldn't be able to beat them on my own. Each attempt had proven just how little I could do. I needed to take this to someone else. It couldn't be Hogget. Going to another gang would lead to more deaths. And if they succeeded, would things be better? It would just end up with a new gang controlling the city.

That left only one other option. Even if they were their lapdogs, the police would be a good option. I'd have to have some form of connections, thanks to my time as Dwight Duncan which could help. If I was smart, I could also force their hands. Well, I didn't know how to spread information online. I knew it was possible. Were I to threaten to get the public involved, the police would have no choice but to step in.

I pushed myself off the sofa. I needed backups, copies, and a hiding spot, and I needed them fast.

It would be a long night.

CHAPTER 17
PATH TO REDEMPTION

My entire body felt like lead as I walked closer to the station. The two cloth bags I had taken were thrown over the shoulder—one of which had the gun that I had dismantled. I'd kept the parts buried underneath the baggies; if an officer noticed the gun when I walked in, things would escalate. But this was for the best—I couldn't do anything on my own and trying to only end up making shit worse.

The doors opened, and I made my way to the front counter. The man was wearing casual clothes, so I doubted he was an officer, though he was fit enough for the job. It was easy to see that his arms were toned even through the long sleeves of his shirt.

I glanced at his name tag. It was still shiny; he was new here. "Hello, Jamir?"

"Good morning, sir. How can I help you?"

"I have a tip about the deaths. They're caused—" I swung the bags around and placed them on the counter. "By this."

Jamir glanced into the bags, and his face took on a greenish hue. He took the bags. "Will you come with me, sir?"

He reached over the counter to put his hand on my shoulder. I let him guide me out of the lobby and into the back, where several uniformed officers were sitting at different desks. A few officers visibly jumped when they saw me, and a few flinched.

A man with gelled-back blond hair started to approach me—the same man who had let me go at Duncan's apartment. I barely took a step toward him when a woman appeared between us. Her brown hair was pulled up in a tight bun at the top of her head. Her uniform was the same as the others, but the markings on the sleeve were different; instinctively, I knew that it was because she was the sergeant.

It was Sergeant Hima Rao. She'd been promoted two years ago after working on the force for 15 years. The whole department had gone out for drinks to celebrate, and I'd gotten drunk on whiskey—I'd been so jealous that I hadn't been given the position instead.

I still couldn't remember my whole life, but I could remember that I was Dwight Duncan.

"Mr. D— *Campbell*." Rao smiled at me, her back straight. "Whatever can we do for you?"

"You know about Dollys?"

Her facial expression didn't change. "I can't say that I do."

I nodded my head toward Jamir, who held the bags out for Rao to see. As soon as she saw the contents, she gestured for one of the officers behind her. The blond-haired man stepped forward and took the bag. As soon as he was gone, Rao turned her attention back to me. "Let's go somewhere private."

She grabbed my arm, and I had to fight back a wince. Even with my right arm being mostly healed, her grip was so strong I was sure that the scabs would break and I'd start bleeding again. Still, I knew better than to fight against her. I let her head me to the side of the room, down the hall, and into the first interrogation room.

It was plain inside—gray walls and floors with a metal table and chairs. One wall had a mirror that I knew was actually a window to the side room. I was pushed down onto one of the chairs, and there I was being put in handcuffs.

"Just a precaution," Rao said. "You understand."

"I came in willingly. I'm not going to run away."

"Maybe. Maybe not. Give me a moment."

Rao turned and left the room. A faint click told me I was locked in. I rested my head against the table and let out a shaky breath. All I could do was hope that I'd done the right thing.

***

I wasn't sure how long the wait was, but eventually, two people walked into the room: an older man with gray hair and a meticulously cared-for mustache and a much younger man with spiked red hair and several tattoos. The older man was wearing a police commissioner's uniform, his badge proudly displayed on his chest, telling me his name was "A. Richard."

The younger man didn't look like an officer, though—he had a red leather jacket covered in silver studs.

While Commissioner Richard stood by the door, the spiky-haired man turned one of the seats around and sat down. He grinned at me, and I knew that I had fucked up.

"So, Mr. Duncan—or should I say Hunter? We heard you got some news for us about Dollys?"

I turned to look at the commissioner. "People are dying because of this stuff."

The man leaned forward and snapped his fingers. "You know, we've gotten some reports in. Apparently, some lunatic with a gun's been running around. Someone attacking people in alleyways."

"They take Dollys, and then they start vomiting. They vomit and vomit until there is nothing left, and then—" The words came out of my mouth even though I didn't specifically remember them happening—"they start hallucinating, thinking it's just the high, experience psychosis until they die."

The commissioner's face was pale. The other man laughed. "You think, what, that they're being poisoned? Be bad for business, don't you think?"

"Just test what I brought in."

"*Or* lock up the man attacking innocent citizens. And, you know, I think we should bring in some of those guys that reported the fire. See if they might remember seeing him around."

"An email is going to go out in two days with everything I've learned." I finally turned to look at the man. "Unless I cancel it."

He stood up and started making his way out of the room. "I need to make some calls."

As soon as the door closed, I turned my attention back to Commissioner Richard. The two of us stared at each other for a while and I could see the moment that his shoulders slumped.

"I appreciate what you're trying to do, Officer Duncan." He reached out and took my hand but wouldn't look me in the eyes. "We will... consider what you've brought to us and do what we can."

He walked out of the room, and I was left alone. I let my head hit the table. I needed to think. My backup plan was still in place, and I still had most of the evidence stashed away, but that didn't mean I wanted to get locked up—or worse. The mirror was too sturdy, so the only way out would be breaking the door. Unfortunately, kicking down doors was loud, and there was no way they'd miss it. Even if I somehow got out, there was still the matter of a whole precinct of officers on the other side.

"Hey!" I called out. "I'm invoking my right to council. I won't talk without a lawyer."

I didn't know if anyone was listening. They could be behind the window, watching, or I could be all alone. I leaned back in my chair and went to cross my arms, only for the handcuffs to stop me.

I was about to start yelling when the door to the room opened to reveal the blond-haired man. He didn't walk in or say anything; just gestured for me to come to him. It could have been a trap, but staying was just as dangerous. If he already got me out of one situation, why wouldn't I trust him to get me out of another one?

With a final glance toward the mirror, I stood up and walked out of the room. The door closed behind me, and the cuffs were removed. I stared at the man's face, but no memories came back.

At least I could finally see his name. "Justin?"

"We need to hurry."

He didn't leave room for me to argue—just grabbed my arm and started moving. For the third time that day, I was powerless. All I could do was hope that Justin would lead me somewhere better than the other two had.

Chapter 18
Resurfacing Memories

The new clothes I was given were two sizes too big and smelled faintly of mothballs. I slipped out of the stall and threw my clothes into the large garbage can. No one looked twice at me as I walked out of the bathroom and through the lobby. I considered leaving once I reached the parking lot, but Justin had pulled up in a car, waiting for me.

I'd barely gotten into the car before Justin started to drive. My one hand stayed on the door handle, with the other was on the seatbelt buckle. If I jumped out at this speed, I'd likely get severely hurt—but that might still be better than wherever he wants to take me. Unfortunately, I wasn't subtle enough.

Justin glanced over at me and clicked the locks on. "Please don't be stupid about this."

"I'm trying to not be."

"And yet you decided to walk *right* into the police station and hand yourself over?"

My grip on the door handle tightened. "The hell else was I supposed to do?"

"Literally anything else? Anything besides walking into the gaping maws of hell—"

"You're being dramatic!"

"Offering yourself up like some kind of sacrificial lamb! You know that you're not alone in all of this—"

I barked out a laugh, but he kept rambling.

"But you go off the map! Had us worried! Thought you'd been compromised!"

"You're still not giving me any better fucking idea!"

"You could have come to me! I thought that would have been obvious!"

"And who the fuck are you?!"

"What is that supposed to mean?!"

"Exactly what I fucking said! I don't know who the fuck you are!"

He went silent. A few blocks later, he started to smack the steering wheel. When he finally calmed down, he pulled the car over. "You really don't remember me?"

I ran a hand down my face. I should have kept my mouth shut. But at least the car was stopped now; it would be easier to escape this way. While I didn't relax, Justin did. He turned toward me and curled up in the seat. His smile was soft, but it didn't reach his eyes.

"Okay. What do you remember?"

"What I need to."

"Dwight. Please." I shook my head, but he ignored me and kept talking. "We didn't have a lot of chances to talk before you were sent undercover. I'd only just been moved to the precinct. And that's why I was your point of contact—no one would suspect that we're connected.

"It worked for a while. You gave me information about their operations. Their plans. And we got the evidence to tag some of them. Then, you started talking about a new drug and... the next thing I know, you went silent. Weren't checking in anymore."

That must have been when I was coming up with the recipe for Dollys and around the time I stopped writing in the notebook. I couldn't remember any of what he was saying though. All I could do was take his word for it—but I wasn't sure how trusting I wanted to be just yet.

"I'm sorry I lashed out. I just... I thought you were dead. And then you walked right into the station, and you were alive, but... the Drogue—"

"What about Hogget?"

Justin frowned. "What about them?"

"How do they tie into all of this?"

He was quick to respond to that. "They don't. Not to Dollys, anyways."

But that didn't make sense. I'd been a member, and they'd killed Dr. Kokoro. Edith had been tied to them, and she'd wanted the notebook. There had to have been a reason I'd been Adam Campbell—that I'd let that bastard clap his hand on my shoulder and pull me up through the ranks.

"Dwight?"

I jumped. Justin's voice pulled me back to the car, and I finally noticed how hard it was to breathe. I brought my hand up to my left shoulder and squeezed. The pain jolted through me; I clenched my teeth against it but didn't let up until I was sure that I was fully present.

To his credit, Justin waited until I had calmed down to speak again. "You may have used them to get information? But that... that wasn't a different investigation. You switched to Drogue because you *knew* they were worse and that nothing was being done about them."

I nodded. I didn't remember the details but it sounded right.

With a sigh, Justin turned back in his seat and started the car again. "Come on. Let's get you somewhere safe."

***

Somewhere safe ended up being his condo. It was a small, modest thing with a perfectly tended garden: a mixture of pink begonia and black dahlias. Apparently, his wife, Kathy, was a big gardener.

I sat in his living room and felt uncomfortable. Though the stray books and used coffee mug gave the place a "lived-in" feeling, the minimalistic style made touching anything feel wrong. It felt like I'd broken or stained the light blue sofa—I couldn't even lean back since it was only a few inches tall. The table was more of a cream-colored block than anything else, but even if it wasn't pretty, it matched the walls. I looked around the room, but besides the flat-screen TV and the lone bookshelf next to it, there wasn't anything else to see.

My leg was shaking as I waited for Justin to come back. When he did, he was holding a large tray filled with a bunch of cheeses, crackers, dried fruits, and rolled-up meats. There were also two large glasses filled with sparkling water and a few floating raspberries.

"Sorry, this was the best I could do last minute."

"Oh, well, if *this* is all you can do." I exhaled before reaching out and grabbing a few meats at random. "So, now what?"

"Well, you've handed over all our evidence which means the only thing we've got on our side is going to be testimonies." Justin reached into his back pocket and pulled out a phone. When he set it down on the table, it was already recording. "So, let's get started. Dwight Duncan, what do you remember?"

I let out a shaky breath before responding, "Not much. Just that... Dollys are dangerous. They're a mix of mollys and LSD, and for some reason, something in the mix makes them die."

"And Drogue? How are they involved?"

"They're the ones making Dollys."

"And what about the police? Are they involved in any way?"

I let out a shaky breath. "Yeah. Drogue sees them as their 'lapdogs.' They know that they won't get thrown in jail."

"How do you know that?"

"I've seen it. They've practically told me."

"But is there anything else? Come on. Think back. Have you seen *any* members of the police force working with Drogue?" I shook my head. The only thing that came close to it was during the car chase and at the warehouse, but if I mentioned that then who knew how quickly I'd get locked up?

Justin stood up and walked over to the bookshelf. He crouched down and stuck his hand through the small gap between the bottom of the shelf and the floor. When he pulled his hand back out, he was holding a piece of paper. He came back and handed it to me.

It was a picture of an older man inside a fancy restaurant. His gray suit made his small frame come across as even smaller. Several liver spots were along the side of his face, which was barely able to distract from his thinning white hair. Despite how fragile he looked, he held himself with confidence. He almost looked like a predator as he ate the steak—the whole plate had been soaked in blood from how raw it was.

But I knew that was how Leon Megalos liked his meat; he'd eaten it that way every time we'd met up to discuss the creation and then the distribution of Dollys. Each meeting had been terrifying but the last one had been even worse when I recognized the mustached man sitting stiffly next to him.

I'd sat through the entire meal, hoping that I'd been insignificant enough for the commissioner to recognize me. I'd thought that maybe I got through it; Richard hadn't said a word, much less looked at me for the whole meeting. But then there was an arm at the back of my neck. I'd been pulled in closer to Megalos, smelled the alcohol on his breath, and been given a choice—hand everything over and stay Jacob Hunter or die.

"Commissioner Richard works with Leon Megalos—the head of Drogue. I saw the two of them in meetings."

"Are they working together to make Dollys?"

"Yes."

Justin reached over and stopped the recording. "Alright. That should be good enough. It won't stop Dollys, but—"

"Then it's not *good enough*. People are dying!"

Justin ran his hand through his hair. "Legally, this is all we can do."

"And what about illegally?"

Justin stared at me for a second before shaking his head. "It would be easier in some sense, sure, but... we'd risk jail time, and I..."

"You can't. I get it. Luckily, only one of us needs to."

CHAPTER 19
THE UNRELATED EPIPHANY

While I had wanted to start planning right away, Justin insisted that he had to get back to the police station before people started to realize that the two of us going missing at the same time were connected. I also needed to hide away inside his condo; he'd emphasized how fucked both of us would be if anyone saw me walking out of his home. The only good thing was that Justin's wife was out of town for a couple of months on some business trip, saving me from having to make awkward conversation.

I tried watching TV to pass the time, and though there were a lot of options, there wasn't anything that could stop my mind from spiraling. I had a rough idea of how the different identities that past-me had were connected, but I still had a lot of questions about "why." Why had I worked to make Dollys? Why had I been willing to meet with Leon Megalos or whoever that fuck is at the head of Hoggets?

And why were people dying? Based on what Phil had said before he left, Dollys hadn't meant to be deadly—they weren't, originally. But I'd seen a young boy dying, and the news made it clear there were more people like him. People were vomiting and dying all over the city because of what I'd done.

I turned off the TV and hurried into the kitchen. The appliances were all new and the counters were almost sparkling from how clean they were. I forced open the fridge and pulled out anything and everything. Everything was put in their own container with a label: fugu, foie gras, and oysters. There wasn't a hint of anything that I'd be able to afford without selling off a kidney.

I had no idea how to cook any of it, but I dug around for a frying pan anyway. I tried to focus on the motions of cutting up ingredients and throwing the things into either boiling water or oil. The smell was horrible, and the final product looked pale and unappetizing. And the entire time I was eating it, all I could think about was Dollys and that final meeting I'd had with Megalos.

Had I taken the deal, I'd have afforded everything that Justin had and more. But I hadn't taken it, and it was not because of fear. I stabbed into the fugu and forced it down. The taste was terrible; I did my best to focus on that instead of the idea that past-me was actually a better person than me.

My hand floated toward the tattoo on my chest—to the three dots. I'd been so sure that I'd been a serial killer; had I even killed anyone before Edith? Though, that was a stupid question when I could still remember the car chase. Two of the three dots were real; over two if I was counting all the Dollys victims. And that wasn't because of what I'd done in the past.

It was all me.

I threw the plate at the floor and it broke. Shards of porcelain mixed with orange oysters and charred flecks of meat and fish coated the tiled floor. I'd need to clean it before Justin got back, but instead, I found myself sitting on the ground. The light shifted in the room. The front door opened. And then, I was being moved up the stairs and gently sat down on a bed.

Justin left the room after that. But it didn't make sense—he wasn't supposed to be back for another few hours. Had I sat there for that long? I let myself fall back into the bed and stare at the ceiling.

A while later, the door to the room opened, and Justin sat down beside me. "Did you want to talk about it?"

I only hummed in response—the sound too one note for even me to understand what it meant.

"Did you... remember something?"

"No." I shook my head. "No, I... guess it just hit me. I'm a piece of shit."

"That's not true." I let out a small laugh, but he kept talking, "I know I only knew you for a little while, but—"

"I don't want to hear about how great I was before all of this."

"Dwight—"

"Just, get the fuck out. Please."

He opened his mouth but said nothing. He stared at me, and then he left.

I held myself back from throwing the pillows. It hadn't been much, but I was so sure that I was at least better than past-me. I'd kept fucking molly in one of my three secret apartments. That had to mean something.

I sat up. I'd had molly in my apartment, I'd tried it, and it hadn't burned; the mix from the warehouse had. "It's something else."

I ran out, down the stairs to the living room. Justin was sitting on the sofa with a laptop, which he slammed shut when he saw me. He moved it to the side and stood up to meet me.

My hands met his shoulders and I stared him straight in the eye. "The Dollys are being altered—they're being specifically made to kill people. But not everyone knows that. They're hiding it from who knows how many people. It's a white powder that burns. If we know what that shit is, then maybe..."

"Okay. Let's me just—" He turned back and grabbed his laptop. "Look... I can only find white phosphorus. But that would burn your eyes and skin just from it being in the air. I can keep looking."

I nodded. I wanted to tell Justin about the safety deposit box where I'd hidden the notebook but I couldn't. Even if each entry was encoded by that stupid atbash code *and* by my inability to write anything that made sense, the idea of it being in anyone else's hands was terrifying. The fact that I was the only one who knew where my "evidence" was, was probably the only reason I hadn't been killed in the interview room. It was also what Edith had been trying to kill me for—what I'd murdered to protect.

I ran my hand down my face and felt the slight bump that was still present on the side of my head. The thought that she'd been a member of Hogget had been dancing in the back of my mind since I'd seen the article about Dr. Kokoro. The hit to the side of her head had been the same as mine, with the only difference being that I'd gotten lucky.

Somehow, Hogget knew that I was keeping records about Drogue, and they wanted that information. If they had it, it wouldn't be long before they figured out where each warehouse was. I couldn't remember if Hogget had guns, but I knew that Drogue did. It would lead to a gang war and a massacre.

"I'm not seeing any other powders like you described."

Even though, barely focused, I nodded. "The lab will figure it out."

"They would, if the samples you brought are actually sent. Though, from what I heard, the redhead took the bags when he left."

"Then, I'll just need to get more."

"We'll add that to our plan then." Justin sighed before closing the laptop again. "A plan that we should talk about. I've done a bit of thinking, and I have an idea. Not about what we should do, but about how. Undercover cops aren't allowed to commit crimes unless they've been given permission. Pardons are also off the table. *But* we can't try a dead person."

"A suicide mission?"

A smile came across Justin's face. "We can work together to make sure that Adam Campbell has a *great* funeral. Unless you're attached..."

"No. Barely knew the man." I let out a small laugh. "So, how are we planning on killing me?"

CHAPTER 20
BREAKING POINT

The cup being placed down next to my head jolted me awake. A tiny pool of drool was crusted onto my face and collecting on the table. I looked around for something to clean it up with when Justin handed me a napkin. It didn't take long to get everything cleaned up or for me to down the cup.

As soon as I'd emptied it, Justin was reaching over to refill my coffee. He offered me a small smile. "I take it this is better than the 'crap from Corners?'"

"Definitely." I swirled the coffee around. "I take it I complained about it a lot?"

"Every time we'd met up there."

I nodded before rotating my shoulder and neck to try and get rid of some of the stiffness. Falling asleep on the table hadn't been the smartest thing I'd done, but it was worth it to have the plan mostly prepared. There'd been countless papers covering the table and floor with even more that had been pushed through the shredder.

As Justin was walking back toward the kitchen, I reached for the TV remote and called out to him, "Is that where we'd meet up to talk about my undercover work?"

"Most of the time. Meeting online would create an obvious trail. But, sometimes, your moaning was enough to force my hand into breaking protocol. You okay with a croque madame?"

"Don't know what that is?" I called out as I turned on the TV.

It was set to some children's show, so I started flipping through the channels. My blood ran cold when I reached the news. The man on the screen was talking about some random fluff piece, but my attention was focused on the text at the bottom of the screen.

The mysterious death count had risen from when I last saw it; seven victims had turned into 30 in just two days. With so many dead, they should have figured out the cause. There wasn't even a mention of the drugs that *must* have been in their system. Why wouldn't they at least warn people about drugs?

A part of me knew that that was a stupid question. I'd seen how easy it was for Drogue to control the police—what was the news in comparison?

I stormed into the kitchen, where Justin was whisking some weird flour and milk concoction. He jumped when he saw me. "Dwight! What?"

"I'm going. We need to start this now."

"What? No. We agreed. Wait for the night shift. The less people, the safer—"

"Fuck that. This has gone on long enough. I'm done!"

Justin stared at me for a moment, his expression unreadable. Eventually, he nodded. "Alright. Any chance we can at least have breakfast first?"

***

I leaned against the back wall of the police station and absent-mindedly played with the set of keys in my hand. The beanie was almost covering my whole face with how far down I'd pushed it. I looked around the corner of the building again, but Justin was still there with that stupid travel mug. A part of me wanted to sneak in and pull the fire alarm, but Justin had been clear that the fire department would arrive in seconds.

Finally, he placed the mug down and walked out of my line of sight. His cough was loud—the actual signal to let me know to start counting. My hand was on the doorknob. Ten seconds had passed, then thirty, and finally one minute. I threw open the door and slipped inside.

The commotion in the front of the office echoed all the way to the back. Justin's plan to start a betting ring was working. It had been clear that the security was shit when I sneaked out the other day, but this made it clear how bad the whole place had gotten. I doubted there was a single person here who gave a fuck.

As angry as the negligence made me, it was working in our favor. I made it to one of the two elevators with no one noticing. The ride down to the basement level only took a few seconds, and so did the walk toward the metal fence that cut off the first part of the floor from the rest. I unlocked the door and went in.

The shelves were inside of the wall and needed a key to be opened. Most of the room was empty—a fact that made the ding of the second elevator even worse. I could go for any of the SWAT team's guns, but there was no guarantee that whoever was coming wasn't armed. Besides, being in here had sparked no memories, if there even were any, so it would be a guessing game. Pulling out a smoke grenade wouldn't help.

There was nothing I could do. The door opened, and I stared at Commissioner Richard. My stomach dropped. With a deep breath, I put my hands into my pockets and began fiddling with the cell phone Justin had given me.

He was calm as he walked toward the cage, but his face looked more aged than it had the other day. "Mr. Duncan."

"Commissioner. Strange place for you to be hanging out."

He let out a small, almost laugh. "Well, it is a problem when one of our suspects managed to escape."

"So, you decide to come and check the equipment room?"

"Mr. Caito's... *display* made it clear that you were planning something. I figured it was this or the evidence locker and, well—" He gestured to the walls. "I didn't want to risk you getting an AK before we could talk."

"About?"

"Why don't we move to—"

"No." I snapped. While there wasn't anywhere for me to go down here, I wasn't going to play along with whatever plan he had. I also couldn't afford to leave without the weapons, not if "Mr. Caito" was Justin. I would not let his whole life be screwed up for nothing.

"There are cameras down here."

Fuck—Justin hadn't mentioned that. "And who are you afraid is watching?"

He winced and hung his head. Even though he looked ashamed, his voice was steady as he spoke. "It is the best for everyone that we don't make a fuss."

"Because that's going so fucking well." I laughed. "So you enjoy being Drogue's lapdog?"

His head shot up, and he glared at me. "As soon as my hands are no longer tied—"

"You'll roll over so they can pet your belly?"

In a second, the commissioner was looming over me. His face had turned red, and his breathing had become heavy. I took it as my chance and kicked.

Despite his age, he was fast. He stepped back and caught my leg. I tried to pull back, but his grip was so tight that all I did was lose my balance. The only reason I hadn't hit the ground was because of the commissioner—I was completely at his will. He said nothing, though. He didn't move. He just waited.

My free leg started shaking, and my knee began to buckle. My concentration shifted for only a second, but that's all he needed. Commission Richard lifted my leg higher before letting go. I tried to catch myself, but I couldn't. Pain seared through my back, and all the air rushed out of my lungs.

When I finally managed to collect myself, I found the commissioner standing over me. "Are you willing to listen now?"

"Fuck off." I rolled over to try and sit up, only to feel a foot slam into my shoulder, forcing me back down.

"Please cooperate, Mr. Duncan. We all want the same thing—"

"As Drogue?"

"As each other. I do not approve of Drogue's methods and would rather not work with them. But..." He sighed. "I learned a long time ago that the laws and justice do not see eye to eye."

"So, you recruited a gang?"

"Of course not!" I felt a hand dig into my shoulder, and suddenly, I was being hoisted up to stare Richard in the eyes. "But when they gave me no other option, I weighed the pros and cons and did what I thought was right."

I spat in his face. "That's what I think of your pros and cons."

"If anyone else were put in charge—"

"What? They'd help create a criminal empire?"

"I'm not—" He pushed me away and started to pace the room. "I have a plan. And it will work."

"How long you've been working on it? A week? Month? Years?" He stopped pacing with his back to me. "If we really want the same thing, then just walk away."

It was quiet for a moment. Then, he cleared his throat. "I can give you thirty minutes, at most, and then I'll be contacting Mr. Megalos to cover up the theft."

He stepped up to the elevators and hit the call button. It was agonizing, waiting for it to arrive, but I didn't want to turn my attention away until I was sure he was gone.

The door closed, and I pulled the phone out of my pocket. I'd gotten the recording started; we hadn't planned on me getting this evidence here, but I would not complain.

Turning to the shelves, I began unlocking everything. Justin would be pissed at me for taking more than we'd discussed, but it didn't matter. I didn't want to go in unprepared if they knew that I was coming. I slipped my sweater off and laid it on the ground—without a proper backpack, it would have to do.

CHAPTER 21
RACE AGAINST TIME

Besides the shitty pop song playing through the radio, the car was silent. Justin was gripping the wheel so tightly that his knuckles had turned white. I caught him glancing into the backseat sometimes. The gun, tasers, and flashbangs were awkwardly packed together under the hoodie. He hadn't commented on it yet, but he was pissed—and he didn't even know about what had happened with the commissioner.

There wasn't an easy way for me to tell him that the police knew we were connected. How do you tell a man that his life was ruined? And it wasn't just his life—his wife's life would, at the very least, be turned upside down. She could be on the run from Drogue as much as we were. We'd fucked everything up.

The song ended abruptly and was replaced by a woman's voice. Even through the terrible audio quality, she was on the verge of tears. "We have an emergency news bulletin. A state of emergency has been issued across the State. A, uh, curfew has been triggered. No, uh, late-night parties. Ha. Um, no staying out past ten p.m. Things will open back up at five the next morning. And, with that, we can... get back to things. I guess."

There was a small click, and then the song that had been playing was restarted. I smacked the side of the car door.

Justin side-eyed me. "It's probably in relation to the numerous deaths."

"No. They know we're coming." As soon as the first part was out, the rest of the story just came out. The more of it Justin learned, the paler he became.

"So, what do we do?"

I glanced at the clock. It was 11:43. There were about ten hours until any stray officer could pull us over. We probably didn't need to deal with the two warehouses I'd already been to: the first had raw materials that would take time to prepare and the second no longer had functioning labs. That left us with five warehouses—two hours for each one. It would also mean that I'd need to reveal the notebook.

"Alright. Here's the deal." I pulled the phone out of my pocket and threw it into Justin's lap. "We're going to split up. I'll take care of the illegal shit. You take the recording from the other day and the one on that phone and figure out how to deal with the police."

"So you're just going to take my car—"

"It would be your car whether you're driving or not."

Justin sighed. "At least let me get back home first."

***

While it didn't take long to grab the notebook from the safety deposit box, sitting in the car trying to decode the warehouse addresses manually took ages. Planning out the best route to take took even longer. By the time I formed some plan, an hour had passed. There would only be about an hour and a half for each warehouse.

I slammed down on the gas pedal and started driving as fast as I could without risking unwanted attention. The entire ride, my mind was going in circles. There weren't enough supplies to go full force into each warehouse. I'd need to be smart and save most of the equipment for the more important warehouses.

The first location was also the first one on the list. It was nothing more than a small storage unit that couldn't be more than $200 a month to rent. The security was also shit. The worker at the front of the building had let me walk around freely when I said I was thinking about getting a unit and wanted to get a feel for the place. The lock had been rusted and easy to break—something that really should have been the first sign this place wasn't important anymore. The stray bits of equipment were easy to break and soon I was heading back to the car to go to the next location.

By the time I pulled up to the apartment building, there were only eight hours left. With four places left, that meant I was back up to two hours per location. I tried to let that information sink in as I grabbed some things from the backseat. A glance inside showed me I didn't need to worry about breaking in; there weren't any locks or way to be buzzed in.

I'd hoped that meant that the security was just as bad, but the bullets that were fired the minute I knocked at the door told me otherwise. I hit the ground and waited for everything to calm down. As quietly as I could, I got into a kneeling position and aimed the taser at the door. I waited for the man to step into my line of sight before pulling the trigger.

The man's body went stiff, and he tumbled to the floor. I switched out the cartridge as I ran past the man. Even though they had done their best to keep the room clean, the age of the building made it nearly impossible. The floors were faded, and the walls were cracked from water damage. But my focus went to the middle of the room where 20 people were set up in some assembly line: one person took out pills and handed them to the next person, who put them in a plastic bag and finally gave it to the third person who placed them in a cloth bag. It was where they got the Dollys ready to sell.

I reached behind my back and pulled out the Glock. With their bodyguard gone, the sight of the gun was enough. Some raised their hands while others cowered behind the table. "Get out."

No one hesitated. I took some time to make sure that the room was clear and then dragged the unconscious man to the stairwell. Back in the apartment, I pulled out the stun gun and the notebook. I ripped out one of the pages and laid it on the table near the cloth bags. It took careful positioning, but I finally lined up the taser with some of the writing I'd done in pencil. The pins went out, and within a few seconds, the fire started. As soon as the cloth bags started to burn, I went over to the other end of the line and began throwing the pills into the fire. Soon, the fire was too much, and I had no choice but to leave—pulling the fire alarm as I went.

There were three warehouses left and six and a half hours before curfew. My heart was pounding in my chest, but I didn't have time to try and calm down. It took 20 minutes to drive to the next place, and my arms had shaken. I took a second to take in the house. It was a nice place in a suburban neighborhood—it reminded me of Justin's condo. But, according to my notes, it was one of the main places that Drogue worked out from.

There were shadows moving around past the windows. It seemed like at least ten people were circling in the front of the house. I cursed; I'd wanted to save as many of the weapons as I could for the actual warehouses, but with this many people, I didn't have a choice.

The M4 carbine was heavy against my back. For a second, I regretted taking it instead of some body armor. But there was no changing things now. I crouched down and ran toward the side of the house. There weren't any open windows around the side or back of the house, and each door was locked. With a deep breath, I stepped back and aimed the Glock.

After a few shots, the window was cracked enough for me to throw the flashbang into the window. As soon as it went off, I jumped in and ran toward the closest wall. The room was some dining area.

Footsteps thundered throughout the whole house—everyone was moving toward me. I'd never be able to take them all out. I took out another flashbang and rolled it through one door before jumping into the other. The hallway I found myself in had no place to hide, forcing me to dive for the closet door. It was an empty bedroom.

I could hear people running down the hall past me. As soon as I was sure it was clear, I hurried out of the room. They were still focused in the dining room, letting me sneak away. From the few glances I had, the first floor was meant to be an *actual* home; I'd need to find the stairs.

As soon as I made it to the second floor, I stared down the two men in suits at the end of the hall. They'd spent an age in the gym—not that they needed it with the handguns in their hands. With nowhere to hide, I had no choice but to aim the M4 at them.

While the man on the left let out a small laugh, the man on the right knocked on the door they were stationed in front of. "Hunter's here, sir."

"Let him in." The voice was muffled, but I could tell it was Megalos.

The man nodded before gesturing me forward. It looked like I had a meeting.

CHAPTER 22
SHOCKING TRUTH

Megalos sat behind an oak desk which had a tea set and sandwiches set up on it. I positioned the gun so it was aimed at him, but he barely even reacted. He gestured toward a small red stool placed against the wall.

I didn't move from where I'd set up against the door of the room, and he sighed. "If we're to have a civilized conversation, you'll need to cooperate with me."

"I think I'd prefer to stay on equal footing, thanks."

"I'm not sure if that is possible, but we can pretend if you wish." He started to pour some of the tea into one of the cups. A sweet, citrus aroma filled the room. "May I offer you some refreshments?"

"Let's just get to the point."

"Yes, I suppose that would be for the best." He took a sip of his drink before twirling the tea around in the cup. "So, Mr. Hunter, let us discuss why you've decided to poison my stock."

I let out an angry laugh. "Pretty sure you're the assholes poisoning shit."

"I see..." He placed the teacup down before leaning forward. He rested his head on his hands and stared at me look I was some specimen. I tightened my grip on the gun. "A shame. That means you're not as smart as I believed."

"The hell—"

"Who is our third party? If you don't mind my asking."

"Hogget" immediately jumped into my head, but I pushed it aside. I couldn't let him fuck with my head.

"Shut up."

He took my silence as a sign to keep talking instead of shutting up. "If you haven't already figured it out, we can try talking it out. I'm sure that I'll be able to pierce it together."

"Shut up."

"I simply want—"

The back of the gun smacked into my shoulder when I pulled the trigger. Even though I stopped right away, Megalos' face was almost unrecognizable. Blood coated the back wall and chair. There was something else, too—something chunky that was stuck all over the place.

That was three kills. Enough to make me a serial killer.

The door striking my back and pushing me to the ground was the only reason I didn't throw up. The men rushed in and toward what used to be Megalos. I moved without thinking, crawling toward the door. I barely got the door closed before the men shook their shock. I wasn't shot through the wall because I was still on the ground.

Footsteps came from the first floor. I removed the last flashbang and threw it down the stairs. The second it went off, I ran down after it. A couple of the men were blindly shooting, but I made it out without getting hit. I slammed the car door and drove as fast as I could.

The traffic around me was awful, and every street seemed filled with more people, but I couldn't slow down. I had to get out.

***

Justin opened the door to the condo in his complete police uniform. He grabbed my shoulder and pulled me inside. The door slammed shut and I could hear the locks being clicked into place. A second later, I was pushed down onto the couch.

"Did you leave everything in the car?"

The Glock felt cold against my back and the notebook was heavy in my pocket. "Yeah, of course."

"Were they hidden?"

"Yeah, of course."

"Alright. Good. I need to get in. I didn't think—" He winced at the sound of yelling from outside. "I need to get in and help with the riots."

"Riots?"

Justin stared at me for a second. "What happened at the warehouses?"

"I killed Megalos."

"You did? That's—" He shook his head, and the voice shifted so that his voice was calm when he continued, "That's alright. It's for the best. It will keep them from being able to recuperate from all their losses. You did the right thing."

I couldn't keep talking about this. "What's going on with the riots?"

"I... I need to get going. Here." Justin turned on the TV before walking over to the door. "I'll handle locking everything up behind me. Don't answer the door or call anyone. Got it?"

I nodded but kept my eyes glued to the TV. There wasn't a reporter on screen—live footage of the streets. There were two hours until the curfew officially started and every part of the city had been filled with people protesting. Government buildings were being vandalized, and even random buildings were being targeted.

The footage of the streets was pushed to the side to make room for the reporter at the station. "We apologize for the delay. We have just received a new report which *confirms* that the whistleblower was correct about Dollys containing high amounts of rat poison.

"Protestors continue to march toward the police station. The investigation ordered by Governor Feld is still ongoing, and Commissioner Richard has yet to issue a statement about the recordings submitted to our station."

My stomach dropped. "We caused this."

I looked up, but Justin was already gone. It was just me now. A flash of orange on the TV caught my attention and I turned to see the live footage shot had switched to an overhead drone capturing footage of a fire.

I grabbed the remote and turned the TV off, but it didn't matter. The sound on the streets was getting louder and closer. I stumbled into the kitchen, where I found Justin's laptop with a cord connecting to the burner phone I'd given him. Seeing it there felt like a punch to the face. No matter where I went, I couldn't get away from the things that I had caused.

"It's okay. It's for the best." The three dots I knew were tattooed onto my chest felt like they were burning. "It's done now. I... I did the right thing."

CHAPTER 23
UNEXPECTED CONCLUSION

It took a month for Justin to let me out of the condo. His wife had never come back—the two had apparently decided that it would be best for her to stay away until the whole thing had blown over.

The riots continued for the rest of the week and got more and more violent. It only stopped because Commissioner Richard had been arrested alongside every other officer with even the slightest ties to Drogue, which had become increasingly violent as members used the riots as cover to take over Megalos' place. It was complete chaos, and the agents from other organizations barely kept everything together. And throughout it all, all I could do was hide away while Justin handled the cleanup.

The countless usage of "Mr. Duncan" hadn't been edited out of the audio I'd secretly recorded in the equipment room— something Justin had apologized for time and time again. He'd apparently only thought to look for his own name. He promised that he'd fix things, even though I told him time and again that I *should* go to jail. But he insisted that I'd done the right thing and that I should be let free. He told me he had a plan.

I walked into the police station and came face to face with Jamir. He offered me a small smile before holding out his hand for my ID. I gave him the Adam Campbell one.

"Alright. I'll need to search you for weapons, but after the pat down, you're free to meet Captain Caito in his office."

I nodded and, a second later, was on my way. Most officers I passed refused to make eye contact with me; none of them wanted to risk looking like they recognized me. While she didn't look at me, my eyes lingered on Rao—she'd been demoted when everything came to light, along with most of the other higher-ups. She'd only been allowed to stay on the force because there had been no signs that she'd been working with Drogue. Still, her life was ruined now.

I found myself outside of the new captain's office. The door was open, revealing the half-put-together space. I knocked, and Justin looked up at me from behind the oak desk. He was still wearing the standard police uniform despite his new position.

"Ah, Mr. Campbell. Welcome. Thank you for coming in on such short notice."

"Of course, sir. You said you... found my cousin?"

"Yes, Mr. Dwight Duncan. An unfortunate tragedy." He stood up from his desk and walked over. "If you'll come with me, I can take you to him."

The morgue was in the building across the street. Again, nobody dared to look at me as we walked toward the elevators. Dwight must have come here a lot for them to also know the truth. Not that I'd ever remember it; the doctor that Justin had got to come in and check on me had said that besides a few memories that may spring up here and there, the amnesia was permanent.

Justin had told me it would be okay, that this just meant that I could start over, but that didn't stop me from feeling terrified.

When we finally reached the body, I almost laughed. I recognized the man—it was the "officer" I had seen in the parking lot when I'd first woken up. Back then, he'd worn a uniform with my real name on it. And now he'd be remembered as me forever; it felt like some big sick joke.

"Yep. This is him. Dwight Duncan."

"Fantastic. Thank you for the help, Mr. Campbell." He put his arm around my shoulder and started leading me back to the elevator. "The coroner will get the paperwork all done for you. Let's get you something to eat."

"Corners?"

"Where else?"

"For someone with such expensive tastes, you sure go to shitty places."

Justin laughed as we got into the elevator. Before he could say anything, his phone started to ring. He held up a finger to me and took the call.

"Hello? Captain Justin Caito speaking."

A woman's voice came through the line—muffled but familiar. I strained my ears, trying to place it.

"It's taken care of, dear. Just like I promised."

Based on his words, it was probably his wife. But my stomach was still in knots. I *knew* that voice.

"I told you that won't be necessary."

Though it stayed calm, the woman raised her voice on the other end slightly. While I couldn't make out what she was saying, I could place it. I felt like I was going to vomit.

"Yes, dear. Okay. I'll keep an eye on it," Justin answered while shaking his head. When he hung up the phone, he smiled at me. "Sorry, just Kathy being... overly cautious."

I swallowed hard. I had to be sure whether Justin knew. "What does she do again?"

"This and that. Mostly project management. But she's not afraid to get her hands dirty if she needs to."

"Like..." I shifted slightly, positioning my hand so it would be easy to grab at his holster. "As a therapist?"

Justin stiffened—not a sign of confusion.

We both reached for his gun, but since I'd been prepared, I got it first.

I pointed it at his head. "You know, I was wondering how the lab managed to get Dollys so quickly. After all, the samples I gave to the police had been taken back."

"Dwight, please."

"It's Hogget. Isn't it?"

"It's better this way."

The shot rang out through the elevator.

I felt nauseated like I had every other time. But that was alright because it was done. I'd done the right thing.

When the elevator door opened, I walked out with my hands up—happy to finally be done with all of this.